SPECIAL EFFECT

By
J. F. BONE

I0541489

ARMCHAIR FICTION
PO Box 4369, Medford, Oregon 97504

*For more information about Armchair Books and products, visit our
website at…*

www.armchairfiction.com

Or email us at…

armchairfiction@yahoo.com

THE STRANGEST SPACE VOYAGE IN HISTORY

His name was Martinelli, and his passion was music. He was also a well-known conductor of classical compositions. Then one day he received the opportunity to conduct the premiere of the greatest symphony ever composed, the "Nine Worlds Symphony" by Nicolai Ilarionovich Raposnikov. Only there was a fantastic catch to it all: He must first obtain original recordings of some of the most bizarre special effects imaginable, which were then to be intermixed with the symphony's final score. Unfortunately, it meant journeying from one end of the Solar System to the other to obtain them. Even worse, the recording of these sounds in some instances was nearly impossible, and in other instances might well result in a horrible death! It was up to a seasoned space captain and his crew to make it all possible—but could they do it in the amount of time they were contractually allotted? More importantly, would they even come back alive?

FOR A SECOND COMPLETE NOVEL, TURN TO PAGE 97

CAST OF CHARACTERS

CAPTAIN LUNDFORS
This indie space freighter operator did strictly small time space runs—until someone offered him two millions credits!

OLAF MARTINELLI
He was a big time classical conductor on a strange quest that would take him back and forth across the Solar System.

BERNSTEIN
"Bernie," as they called him, was tough as nails and willing to put his life on the line for his captain and fellow crewmen.

BELLINI
All he knew about Venus swampsuckers was that they had devoured his brother—and he wanted them all dead!

NALTON
He was just a green kid, but he had a genial spirit that made him a real booster to morale on a trip to the end of the Solar System.

LOR T'SHONKE
All this Martian religious acolyte had to do to attain priesthood was pass a simple test—but failure meant losing his ears!

ANDERSON
He said he'd be able to get a recording of a Coren war cry—no problem. But it got him a lot more than he bargained for.

CHAPTER ONE

YOU'VE heard the 'Odalisque', I expect," Martinelli asked.

"Who hasn't?" I said.

"Raposnikov at his best," he said, "and his best is very good indeed."

"There's no one like him, past or present," I enthused. "Nicolai Ilarionovich Raposnikov was the finest composer who ever lived, his handling of special effects alone would make him great but his intimate understanding of music, his feeling for balance and harmony, his exquisite employment of modern technology and ancient art to produce music that can be felt and sensed, as well as heard, why—there's never been a composer who could compare—" I sputtered, losing my eulogy in my enthusiasm.

You might gather from this outburst that I like music— and you'd be right—although to look at me you'd hardly figure it. Spacemen look like what they are—Muscle Beach boys with a prison pallor. We're an anachronism on an Earth welded to the twenty-hour week and balanced caloric diets. Compared to the slim bronzed groundlings, we sailors stand out like Charolais bulls in a herd of Angus heifers. Some of us try Mantan to blend in with the general background but we never manage to make it. Our eyes give us away. You can't spend months on end looking for trouble without developing a certain restlessness of the eyeballs that refuses to let one's vision linger too long upon any one object; "Dancing Eyes" the groundlings call us. They give us our character and part of our reputation. We're the last of the pioneers, our direct ancestors are the sailors, the conquistadors, and the mountain men who opened up the western hemisphere back in the Dark Ages. In short, we're romantic hellers.

The only trouble, as far as I'm concerned, is that I don't want to be a romantic heller. Sure—I like women—but I'd rather spend, an evening at Berlino's eating a good steak than taking a two-minute break at a Calorie Counter. I'd rather sit in Carnegie Hall listening to good music than sweating at Roseland dancing to squirm. And while it's fun to kiss a girl goodnight, I have no desire to have her cluttering up my apartment until the following morning. As far as I'm concerned, I'd rather live back in those quiet days of the middle Twentieth Century than in these hectic ones of the middle Twenty-second.

I sighed and let my gaze flicker over the dark man who sat across the table from me. His name was Olaf Martinelli and he was a conductor. He'd been on the podium at Carnegie several times when I was in the audience. He wasn't bad—at times he was even great, but he had a poor reputation in upper music circles. He was a glory-grabber, a tyrant, a disciplinarian of the old Toscanini school, and about as trustworthy as a Venerian swampsucker on a hot day. I didn't like him by reputation, and his personality wasn't much better. He was too dark, too tall, too smooth, and too well informed about my habits. He had looked me up, run me down, and cornered me in Eddie's Bar, where I occasionally stop for a drink. He'd been thoroughly briefed, except that he didn't know I distrusted tall, smooth characters, and that I have no faith in artists as businessmen. Any day I'd rather take a chance with a hardheaded contractor than an artist. Painters, actors, musicians—they're all alike, people who usually have their feet firmly planted on a cloud. Once I was soft enough to freight an entire musical comedy group to Mars, which was a mistake since the company went broke and I couldn't sell their contracts for beans. Bad artists are a glut on the Martian market, and I wasn't about to get in another jam like that. By sticking to regular business I manage to run a fairly profitable operation, I own the *Virgin Queen* and I intend to keep on owning her. I'm not eager to take on speculation charters or cargo. Let the guys who are riding high do that! Small operators like me have to stick to hard cash and let the big chances go by. We never make millions but we stay alive and do what we like to do—which is travelling the spacelanes.

MARTINELLI, however, had a proposition. He leaned forward across the table and tried to hold my shifting blue eyes with his protuberant brown ones. "You're just the man I've been looking for," he said. "A spaceman who appreciates good music. You're a rarity, my friend, a rarity."

"What's so odd about liking music?"

His eyebrows rose. "Have you ever considered the statistical improbability of finding an independent spacer who understands and appreciates Beethoven, Tchaikovsky, Dvorak, Moussorgsky, Sibelius, Taylor, Shostakovich, Callendar, Rachmaninoff, Bax, Debussy, and Rostanzo?"

"Not to mention a few others," I added helpfully.

He nodded. "Actually, Captain Lundfors, you're unique. And you're precisely the man I have been looking for."

"How's that?"

"Would you like to charter your ship for a year's cruise?"

I gulped. A year's charter would get my pint-sized operation solidly on its feet. I could buy some needed tube liners and insulation. I could have the *Virgin Queen* dry-docked and thoroughly overhauled. I could clean up the back-pay accounts of my crew. I could buy myself a new uniform to replace the threadbare grays I was now wearing. A year's charter would be a dream.

"It would cost you plenty," I said.

"How much?"

"Two million credits."

Martinelli winced. "What does that rocket of yours run on—gold?" he asked.

"Plutonium. It's more expensive."

"I didn't realize these things cost so much," Martinelli's voice was flat. "I don't think I can afford it."

"I might be able to shave the costs a little," I said dubiously, "but a year's cruise can be damned expensive. It depends on where you want to go. Incidentally, where *do* you want to go?"

"Hmm—let's see—Mercury, Venus, Mars, Titan, Io, Callisto, Ganymede, and—oh yes—Pluto."

"All the inhabited worlds in the system!" I said. "Why?"

"I'll tell you that if we can come to terms," Martinelli said. "Until then, that's my secret."

"We can dicker," I said, "but it won't be much less than two million—not with an itinerary like that. Or do you realize that it will take you nine months of that year just to travel to those places? Pluto's a long way out, and Mercury's pretty close to the sun. Frankly, it's a cheap price."

He shook his head. "I don't know," he said. "I'm not a poor man but that's pretty steep."

"Tell you what we can do," I offered helpfully. "After we check your credit rating, we can go down to Univac Center and put the problem up to the computers." Actually I'd do that anyway before I ever made a smoothie like Martinelli a firm offer. "We'll figure it as cost of operation plus ten percent. That ought to be fair enough. You lay out the itinerary and I'll insert the *Queen's* latest operating data. We add ten percent to that, and if you're willing to go on from there, I'm your man."

"That sounds fair enough," Martinelli said.

"Of course," I added, "there'll be the usual demurrage, port charges, change of destination clauses, *and* an Act of God clause included in the contract."

Martinelli looked at me with a faint light of respect in his bulging brown eyes. "You don't miss a bet, do you?" he asked.

"I've been dealing with contractors for twenty years," I said dryly.

He laughed, and I chuckled with him.

"I'll file our contract in Public Archives," he said, "providing we agree on one. Some day it'll be a historical document."

It was my turn to laugh. "Do you think they'll accept it?" I asked. "What sort of business would make a freighter's contract a public record?"

"Wait," Martinelli said. I shrugged.

THE basic figure Univac gave us was two million, one hundred and thirty thousand, five hundred and twenty-seven credits. Martinelli whistled with dismay. "I should have taken your original offer."

"It wasn't firm," I reminded him, thinking as I did that computers were almost as easy to fool as conductors. With new tube liners in the *Queen* I could shave half a million off that figure. But Univac didn't know that. It had to work upon the data I had given it, and new high performance tube liners weren't included in that data. For two hundred thousand I could have the *Queen* docked, relined and refitted. I would be getting the equivalent of a new ship and nearly three hundred kilocredits to boot.

"The other figures I've checked were all about the same as yours," Martinelli said glumly, "except for IPC. That bunch wanted three million."

"Interplanetary has newer and faster ships," I said. "And, besides, they're a big outfit."

"I don't need a big outfit," Martinelli replied. "Yours will do nicely. Now let's go up to my office. We'll have a law firm make up the contract. And then I'll tell you what I want you to do."

"You won't mind if I select the lawyers?" I asked.

He shook his head. "You can hire the Attorney General if you wish." He sounded indifferent.

"Akers, Callahan, Weintraub, and Kabele'll do well enough," I said. "They've handled my freight contracts for the past decade."

"They're a good firm," he agreed. "I've done business with them once or twice on tour contracts."

I looked at my copy of the contract and nodded. As far as I could see it was fair enough. It had the usual penalty clauses for nonperformance, but essentially it was a standard freight contract. I agreed to deliver Brother Martinelli and such equipment as he would bring with him to the eight inhabited worlds of the Solar Union. The order in which the worlds were to be visited was at my discretion. The only bad feature was the time element. One year was all I had to complete the trip. And that wasn't too much time. One minor accident, one bad touchdown, could ruin me. But I had fulfilled worse contracts than this one and I had no cause for complaint. I knew the *Queen* inside out and was perfectly aware of what she could and could not do. This job she could handle.

"All right," I said. "Now what are we making this trip for?"

"To collect sounds," Martinelli said.

"Sounds!"

"Remember we were talking about Raposnikov?"

I nodded.

"You'd really have to know the man to appreciate this, but Nicolai Ilarionovitch Raposnikov was a Unionist all his adult life—and when the Solar Union was established, he decided to write a symphony honoring it. He finished it just before he died last year. It is his masterwork, his greatest production, the piece toward which his entire life was directed. It's called the *Nine Worlds Symphony* and is dedicated to the Solar Union." Martinelli looked at me, his brown eyes glittering. "It's probably the most valuable single piece of property in existence today," he said. "And I own it on condition that I present the entire score *exactly as it was written* in its debut on the tenth anniversary of the Union. And that date is a year and a half away."

"Then why are you hiring a space ship?" I asked. "It seems to me that you'd be hiring a symphony orchestra."

"It's not that easy," Martinelli said. "You see, Raposnikov took a leaf out of Tchaikovski's book, only he went one step farther."

"Tchaikovski?"

"Remember the 1812 Festival Overture?"

I nodded. "The one with the special effects?" I asked. "The cannon, the Moscow bells, and the brass band?"

"That's the one. Well—Raposnikov out-Tchaikovskied Tchaikovski. His piece calls for a steam hammer working a steel ingot, a Dixieland Jazz Band, a spaceship taking off, the sound of the lava flows on Mercury's twilight zone, the bellow of a Venerean swampsucker, the temple bells at K'vasteh, the Corens' war cry, the nesting call of a flock of Ionion Kalliks, Callistan whistlers, a hegemon, and a Plutonian ice fall. Oh, yes, and the sound of a hulled spaceship."

"That's quite a mess of sound," I said. "I've been on the spacelanes for twenty years, and I've yet to hear a Callistan whistler or a Kallik's nesting call. Never was on any of the outer worlds except Ganymede, but you should have no trouble there. A hegemon's easy to dicker with. For that matter, I've only heard a swampsucker just once—and, frankly, I don't want to hear one again. Those subsonics play hell with the nervous system."

"I tried to get the sounds from the Solar Union Academy," Martinelli went on, "but they're not recorded. You'd think they would be," he added aggrievedly. "It just goes to show that when you want something out of a museum you can't get it. They've got plenty of stuffed Kalliks, and whistlers, and even a stuffed swampsucker, but not a single sound." He shrugged. "And since the contract states that original sounds must be furnished, I'm stuck with an exploring job."

"How much is the Academy offering for a copy of your soundtrack?" I asked.

Martinelli smiled wryly. "Not much, just the technicians, professional guides, and the recording apparatus."

"That should be quite a saving."

"It would be except for one thing. I have to pay them for every soundtrack over five, and I'm not sure they'll record the proper key and pitch I'll need to fit into the symphony."

I shook my head. Martinelli had a job ahead. I wondered why he took it, and said so.

"You haven't heard the *Nine Worlds*," Martinelli said, "otherwise you wouldn't ask. You want to hear it ?"

I nodded. Raposnikov is one of my favorite composers.

MARTINELLI opened his desk safe and took out a roll of recording tape. "I had this made in sections," he said, "so no one would be able to copy the theme. Some of the sounds are in already—the first movement is complete; so you can get an idea what the finished piece will be like." He pressed a button and a panel on top of his desk slid aside to reveal a modern stereo—one of those fancy jobs with acoustical depth. He threaded the tape and placed his finger on the starter button.

"The first movement," Martinelli said quietly, "deals with man's conquest of space. Unlike Dvorak's *New World* the shape of the main subject is introduced directly. There is no hinting, no intimation of things to come. It is more like Beethoven's Fifth—a direct, demanding introduction that draws the listener bodily into the vigorous *Allegro molto* with its hypnotic repetitive rhythm. The theme is advanced by a transition that is actually a subsidiary theme in F-minor played first by the flutes and oboes and picked up by the other woodwinds and strings. The second main theme is carried by the brasses in G-major, starting with a muted trumpet playing an unmistakable derivation of Rosinski's *Space and the Atom.* The harsh, almost militaristic note is augmented by the brasses, modified by the wood-winds and swept to a glittering crescendo by the strings and kettle drums, culminating in the hissing roar of a spaceship's jet with their supersonic overtones that are almost painful— listen!" He pressed the button.

I was relaxed, soothed by Martinelli's summation, and utterly unprepared for the violent opening as the full orchestration of over two hundred pieces hammered at my eardrums. It was a blockbuster opening, something that would have made Beethoven turn green with envy. It was Raposnikov all right, but a Raposnikov I had never heard nor dreamed of hearing. The music picked me up, hurled me into a world of sound and fury, of men and metal and dreams turned into steel and atomics. It was pure sensation—music that made me want to laugh and weep, to swell with pride, to suffer the heartbreak of failure and to feel the grim determination that next time—next time we would succeed.

For a few minutes, I was a part of all mankind who ever dreamed of the stars. My chest hurt, my brain throbbed, and cold involuntary chills ran down my spine. My legs trembled, and tears actually came to my eyes at the termination when man finally achieved his ancient dream and left earth for those glittering witch lights in the heavens. The sounds, as Martinelli called them, were an integral part of the theme. Their presence was essential. From steam hammer to jet-blast, the sounds were a part of the music, complementing it, augmenting it, making the whole, movement the vital, living, striving thing it had to be.

Martinelli stopped the tape, and I relaxed, shivering with reaction.

"My gawd…" I said weakly. "I thought I had heard them all, but this is incredible!"

"See what I mean," Martinelli said. "This is the greatest thing that man has done in music. Ownership of this score is literally worth millions. And I own it if I can reproduce it precisely as Raposnikov wrote it. Do you wonder why I am willing to spend over two million chartering your ship?"

"No," I said. "And if the rest of that symphony is like the beginning, I'd almost be willing to donate the *Queen* to help you pull it off." I was drunk with sensation. Never in my life had I heard such music.

"Almost," Martinelli chuckled, "but not quite—eh?"

I sighed, shrugged, and stood up. "A man must live," I said, "and space is my life and the *Queen* my home. There are things like fuel, repairs, wages, and dockage charges. Those cost money and, unfortunately, I'm not a rich man."

"But you love music," Martinelli said, "so you will be eager to help me."

"That's about it," I said.

"And that is all I will need to make this debut a success," Martinelli said. "I thank you, Captain Lundfors." He held out his hand.

I gripped it. It was I who should be thanking him, I thought. He had given me a taste of glory.

CHAPTER TWO

A WEEK later the *Virgin Queen* was ready for blastoff. Port Maintenance had completed a man-killing crash program in record time, and the *Queen* was as tight and true as the day she left the ways. For the first time in years everything aboard the old girl worked as it should. I collected my crew from the fleshpots of New York and Westchester, herding the grumbling spacemen aboard like a father loading his children into the family car at the end of vacation. Three weeks liberty on full pay and the men still complained. They hadn't had it so good in years but they wanted more. Of course they didn't get it, since a contract is a contract, and a spaceship captain is God Almighty as far as his crew is concerned.

About the only man who looked happy about coming back was Egon Bernstein, my executive officer. Bernie was old enough to appreciate space. The rest—mostly four-year men—were hardly dry behind the ears. I wasn't too happy with them, but with the major spacelines giving two-year contracts and bonuses to experienced men with six or more years of service, an independent freighter has to take what's left and be thankful it is no worse.

The Solar Union boys—five of them—arrived with a truckload of sound equipment, which they supervised like mother hens guarding chicks. They stored their equipment with meticulous care, took their shockcouch assignments, and fitted into the ship's routine with the ease of professional space travelers.

Martinelli and two heavy-shouldered men showed up with another pile of gear, which we stowed. We took on last minute supplies, extra fuel slugs for our reactor, and topped off the chemical tanks with nitric and hydrazine. I checked the stations from the control chair, got the all clear signal from the tower, and blasted off.

Outside the atmosphere shell of Earth I cut the chemicals and switched on the atomics. A pale blue glow spurted from the drive tubes as we began to pile on velocity for the long trip to Pluto. I had checked our possible courses at Port Astrogation and had finally decided that the relative positions of the planets were such that the outer worlds offered the best positional relationships—and when we had finished with them, the inner worlds would be in good juxtaposition if we could keep to the schedule I had planned.

The outward trip was fortunate. We picked up a thumb-sized meteorite as we crossed the asteroid belt and the crash and hiss of escaping air were satisfactorily recorded by the Solar Union men, I gave them plenty of warning to get set up and although I could have used the screens to deflect the tiny chunk of metal, I figured that if we could get a meteor strike recording this early in the game we were all to the good.

Damage control quickly repaired the leak as the soundmen checked their tapes with Martinelli.

"Did you know your hull rings in F-sharp?" Martinelli asked me as he came into the control room during the first watch after the collision. He had gotten over his space sickness quickly and was continuously active—nosing through the ship, asking questions of the crew, Bernie, and myself, and behaving like a rubbernecking tourist. In a way it was laughable, but somehow I couldn't laugh at Martinelli. The man was too intense, too serious to be a comic figure.

"Is that good?" I asked.

"It's perfect. That passage was written in F-sharp. We won't need to try again or make tonal adjustments. We have a recording that'll turn the public's hair when we use it. It's great! And that young crewman yelling 'Meteor strike!', that was the convincing touch."

"You mean Nalton?" I asked.

"Yes, that's his name."

"He's young," I said, "young and pretty green. Making, a planet out of an asteroid. He should have kept his mouth shut. But maybe it's a good omen. When a goofur turns out all right that's a good sign."

"I never thought you were superstitious," Martinelli said.

"All spacemen are superstitious," I replied. "I guess it's because space is so big and we're so small."

"When are we due to hit Pluto?" he asked.

"If we've laid the course right—in about two months."

"Long time."

"Long distance—Pluto isn't just next door."

"I realized that, but I didn't realize what it'd be like cooped up in here with only a thin metal skin between us and space. Frankly, that meteorite had scared me."

I grinned. "I didn't feel so good either—and we almost took it in the screen control, which would really have made things sticky. Without screens we'd be in bad shape."

"Would it be that serious?" he asked worriedly.

I smiled without humor. "We finished one run from Mars to Earth without screens," I said, "and we ran out of patches. There were one hundred and thirty-seven holes in the *Queen's* skin. We looked like a sieve, finished the trip in space suits, and had two casualties."

He shuddered. "I hope the screens hold this time."

"They will," I assured him. "The generators have been completely rebuilt."

CHAPTER THREE

I WISH Raposnikov had had a better understanding of the technical details of sound transmission," Martinelli said bitterly as we stood on Pluto's icy surface and surveyed the frozen desolation about us. "Just how are we going to record an ice fall on a world without atmosphere?"

"There's plenty of atmosphere," I replied as I scuffed the blue-white dust underfoot with an insulated space boot. "The only trouble is that it's all frozen—liquid helium, solid oxygen, nitrogen and carbon dioxide. What would you expect on a world three and a half billion miles from the sun?" I was angry with myself. I should have realized that Pluto's solid and semi-solid atmosphere was incapable of transmitting audible sound. We had our two and a half-month trip for nothing.

All about us were the giant glaciers that covered Pluto's surface, knife sharp jagged blocks of ice rising hundreds of feet into the air, cold and black under the faint light of the stars and the tiny disc of the sun low on the horizon. The radome of Pluto Station bulged darkly behind us and a little to one side were the clustered spikes of the station spaceships and the bulkier mass of the *Queen* standing on her landing pads.

Far below our feet in tunnels and corridors carved from the endless ice, the men and women of Pluto Station went about their daily tasks—adaptable as only humans can be—carving a life and living out of the frozen crust of the ice world.

"Obviously Raposnikov was thinking of the icefall of '98," I said. "The one in the main lateral of the old station. There was air down there—and there was undoubtedly sound."

"That could be it," Martinelli agreed. "Let's go below. It's getting cold up here."

I had to agree with him. Despite the insulation and heating elements of our spacesuits, the frightful cold of Pluto was seeping through my boots and the joints of my armor. I turned toward the station's airlock, the chilled joints of my armor somewhat stiffer than normal, and as I turned I cast one flickering glance around the horizon. It was purely habit—the trained eye reflex of a spaceman—but in that brief glance my vision caught an abnormality. One of the tall ice spires above us was distinctly wrong. No longer vertical, the tall black tower was leaning outward, toppling with silent ponderous deliberation.

"Icefall!" I yelled. "Run!"

Martinelli's reflexes were as fast as my own. He cast one lightning glance upward and then broke into a clumsy run for the steel and cryoplastic revetment that guarded the station entrance. I pounded along behind him. In Pluto's light gravity we made surprisingly good time despite the armor that encased us. As we dove for the shelter of the revetment, the airless sky of Pluto was filled with hurtling shards of ice as the pinnacle struck and shattered. One small piece struck me in the ribs while another ricocheted off Martinelli's helmet. Two years ago he'd have been a dead man breathing space through a shattered helmet, but the ice shard merely glanced off the tough cryoplastic without doing any harm.

Well—almost no harm. Martinelli was scared to death, but that was all. Apparently he had read some of the old stories about what happened when something hit a helmet.

"You're okay," I assured him as I lifted him to his feet.

"My helmet?"

"New model," I grunted. "They don't shatter nowadays."

"Thank God! For a minute I thought I'd had it," Martinelli said. His voice was unsteady. "I don't want to die—at least not until I've produced the *Nine Worlds*."

"My personal opinion is that all conductors are born to be hung, so you're safe until you get back to Earth."

"Not funny," Martinelli said, but he chuckled just the same. Occasionally it takes a bit of graveyard humor to draw the iron out of hiding. He was all right now. "You know, it's too bad that Pluto has no free air. That could have been a wonderful sound."

"The only sound I want to hear right now is the bubbling of a coffee pot," I replied.

"You have a point there," he said, as he helped me open the small airlock.

WE CHECKED with Herb Hallowell, the station superintendent, about the possibility of air remaining in the old station. "The Old Station? Hmmm. I don't know. We abandoned that place nearly fifty years ago. Why do you want to go there?"

"I don't," I said, "but Mr. Martinelli does."

"I want to record an icefall," Martinelli said. "And since there's no atmosphere outside—".

"There's no sound," Hallowell interrupted. "But why do you want to record an icefall?"

"I think I'd better explain," Martinelli said. "In a year and a quarter, Earth time, the Solar Union centennial is going to occur and we're going all out to make it one of the greatest shows Earth has ever seen. Part of the program is a sound recording of typical noises of the nine inhabited worlds, and an icefall is typical of Pluto."

Hallowell grimaced. "It's typical all right. Well—you can visit the Old Station if you wish but I won't be responsible for your safety."

"Is there an atmosphere?" Martinelli asked.

"There was the last time anyone visited the place."

"When was that?"

"Five years ago."

"Hmmm—that means there's probably some left."

"There should be. Ice is pretty good insulation."

We left for the Old Station the next day. Five of us—Martinelli, myself, Nalton, and the two heavy-shouldered apelike men Martinelli had brought along from Earth. Their names were Anderson and Bellini—which had become shortened naturally to Mr. A. and Mr. B., and finally to Able and Baker, during the long trip out to Pluto. Although most of the crew understood the inference, I'm sure that neither Able nor Baker did. It was one of those sly spacemen insults that often resulted in broken skulls when the victim realized what it meant, but in this case I doubted if it would. The simian resemblance of Able and Baker extended to their mental capacity if not to their sex. They were a pair of good-natured brutes, capable of shaking your hand or cutting your throat with the same friendly smile on their face. Martinelli called them guides, but goons would probably have been more accurate. Able had prospected on Titan and Baker was a Venerean swamp rat, but neither of them had any experience on Pluto. Still, their muscles were handy for lugging heavy equipment, and we could use them.

We took along some of the high-priced recording equipment to get the sound of an icefall if an audible one could be made available, and a few explosive charges to make one available if nature wouldn't cooperate.

The Solar Union men refused to come unless Martinelli paid them, and Martinelli refused to pay for such a simple thing as this sort of recording. They were within their rights. Pluto wasn't included on their agenda but I couldn't blame Martinelli. After all, a technician's pay on a hazardous mission isn't peanuts and Martinelli had already laid out quite a bit of change for this trip. So we left them behind to enjoy the warm comfort of Pluto Station while we did the work.

The station rolligon carried us to the old airlock of Station One. The antique double lock was still functioning, and the dials on our spacesuits indicated a two-thirds Earth normal atmosphere inside. They didn't indicate that the air was breathable, and we weren't about to take any chances since we had twenty hours' supply in our tanks. I had brought Nalton along to help us. The youngster was the only one of us who had more than a speaking acquaintance with explosives. He had taken a course in field demolitions and derelict removal at the Space Academy and planned to start his own business as a spacelane contractor in the asteroid belt as soon as he finished his course in practical spacemanship on the *Queen*. Nalton was a nice kid—the clean-cut Academy type that look as though they had been stamped out of a mold labeled "Made in Alamogordo." But some of that Academy veneer was wearing off. He had a sense of humor, a quick wit, and a quick tongue. He learned fast and was well liked. Some day he'd be a first class spaceman. But it was his knowledge of explosives that made him a member of the party.

Inside, the supports holding the ice roof were warped and twisted from the slow flowing of the ice, and the broad tunnel into the depths that had once been straight was now crooked and bent. Our lights cast beams of brightness ahead of us as we cautiously made our way downward to what had once been the entrance hall from which passages had radiated outward to the various working and living levels. The hall was barely two-thirds its former size, its walls oddly twisted and warped. It looked fragile and unstable. Many of the supporting girders were buckled and useless. A great pile of broken ice lay on the floor, evidence of an icefall that could have happened years—or minutes—ago.

Martinelli looked up at the jagged ceiling some ten meters overhead. "This will do," he said. "There's plenty of free drop here to get the crash and rattle that will be necessary. We can plant the microphone in the entrance and bury a couple of small charges under that bent pillar in the center of the room and see what happens when we touch them off."

"Nalton," I said.

"Yes, sir."

"You're the demolitions man. What'll happen if we crack that pillar?"

Nalton looked upward. "It'll probably bring the whole roof down," he said. "That hunk of duralloy is supporting about half the load on the center of the ceiling."

"How much plastic do you figure's necessary for the job?"

"About four hundred grams, sir. I wouldn't care to use any less."

"Well—get about it," I said, "and be careful. In air as cold as this, plastic's tricky stuff so I've been told."

"I know, sir," the youngster said. "That's why I've been keeping it in a thermo bag. It should be hot enough to mold easily."

"Okay, it's your baby. Get the charge placed. I'll run the detonator wires back to the entrance. When you're through, come up and join us. Then we'll set it off. Martinelli and his two monkeys'll handle the sound recording."

Nalton grinned, and I hoped that Able and Baker didn't get the drift—but it was hardly probable that they would, I dropped the end of the wire beside Nalton and slowly climbed the long corridor to the surface, paying out carefully and doing my best to avoid the leads Martinelli had run from his microphones. When I arrived at the airlock, the three of them had already set up the recorder and had the tape running.

MARTINELLI looked up at me. "Thought I'd better get this going just in case," he announced cheerfully.

"Just in case of what?"

"You never know. That hall looked pretty fragile to me. That ceiling could come down any minute."

"Nice cheerful guy, aren't you?" I asked. "Or do you know Nalton's down there?"

"I know and it worries me, but this is the only place we'll get an audible icefall on this crazy world. There's no sense in missing anything."

As though in answer, the needles on the recorder jumped clear across the dial faces and a shudder rippled upward through the ice.

"Icefall!" Martinelli yelped.

"Nalton!" I shouted—and started down the passageway. A blast of frigid air swept up out of the depths and a whole section of passage in front of me buckled, twisted, and with horrid deliberation broke into huge blocks and shards that filled the passage with flying daggers! I stumbled back. There was sound this time, rumbling, grinding sound as millions of tons of ice shuddered, shifted, and crushed together. The shock wave from the ice-quake knocked me to my knees. Blind with panic I turned and crawled back to the airlock as shock after shock rippled through the cracked and shattered ice. Martinelli and the others were already standing outside, numbed by the violence of the quake, uncertain whether to run or stand still. The rolligon had been tossed nearly two meters from where we had parked it, and stood rocking back and forth on its flotons as the tremors passed with steadily decreasing intensity as the shifting ice obliterated the last trace of Old Station—and spaceman second class Tamashiro Nalton.

I felt numb. Five minutes ago Nalton was alive—a nice kid with a sense of humor and a future. Now—my mind recoiled from the thought of what those millions of tons of shifting ice had done to him.

Martinelli, Able and Baker looked at me. Martinelli's face was frozen in horror—the two goons merely looked stupid. But one thing I was thankful for, they weren't grinning. If they had so much as showed a tooth I think I'd have killed them. I liked Nalton. The boy was a morale lifter. We were all going to suffer from his loss.

"I hope you got your damned sound," I gritted as I faced Martinelli.

He shivered and a measure of sanity came back to his eyes. "Oh gawd!" he said. Sweat stood out on his high forehead. "I've never heard anything so horrible—and Nalton's screams!" He retched—something that no one should ever do in a spacesuit—and I could no longer see his face.

SOMEHOW I managed to get Able and Baker moving. We packed the recording apparatus, led Martinelli back to the rolligon and headed back to Pluto Station across the ice hills that separated the old from the new base. I let Martinelli stew in his own digestive juices. At the moment I could do nothing else—and perhaps even if I could I wouldn't. I couldn't help blaming him for Nalton's death, and every time I thought of that grinning cheerful kid I felt sick and angry— angry as much at myself as at Martinelli, I should never have let a man of mine go down into that death trap. Getting the sounds was Martinelli's business, not mine or my crew's. Next time—and all the rest of the times, he could damn well kill his own sloats.

CHAPTER FOUR

WE BLASTED off Pluto in a somber mood. Martinelli with his burned face, me with my guilt and resentment, the crew with their anger at the Solar Union technicians, and the technicians with their righteous air that was all the more sickening because it was right; They didn't have to go on that trip that killed Nalton. The *Queen* wasn't a happy ship as we hurtled sunward to intercept Saturn. Not even the fact that the recording of the icefall was better than Raposnikov could have wished helped very much. I couldn't listen to it. The scream torn from Nalton's throat just at the beginning was all I could take.

We orbited Saturn on schedule, and the sight of the great, ringed world spinning below us was as heartening to the crew as a shot of euphoral. You could feel their spirits rise as we drove in toward the rings, killing our speed to make a landing on Titan.

Like Pluto, Titan was an ice-world. Its surface temperature of minus 245 degrees centigrade was far too low to support unprotected human life, but it wasn't too low to support the Corens, those peculiar amorphous entities with their silicon-based organic structure and their incredible capacity to withstand cold. Like most of the sun's natural children that man had visited, the largest moon of Saturn supported life. Pluto, the captive planet with the eccentric orbit did not. Nor did Iapetus or the smaller airless satellites of Jupiter and Neptune. But Titan, with its atmosphere, was inhabited long before man came to share the world and plunder it of its natural resources of heavy metals. The Corens, semi-intelligent, partly civilized, and thoroughly unpleasant, had done their best to discourage immigration, and had succeeded remarkably well until the First Punitive Expedition reduced them to relative harmlessness.

They still attacked isolated prospectors now and then, but they stayed away from the domes where Earthmen worked and were present in numbers. They had learned their lesson and were no longer a menace. A nuisance, perhaps, but mankind was big enough to withstand nuisances, and we had no intention of committing genocide upon the original inhabitants. We had no use for the frigid surface of their world. Our interests lay in what was under the surface—the uranium, the thorium, and the other heavy elements that powered Earth's atomic civilization. So there were probably as many Corens today as there were when the first prospectors arrived, and they were still the wild, warlike, death defying savages who would willingly sacrifice a hundred of their number to kill one human. The only difference between the modern Coren and his ancestors is that he didn't care to commit fruitless suicide attacking domes and spaceships.

"Just how," I asked Martinelli, "do you expect to get a recording of, a Coren war cry? They avoid us."

"Simple," Martinelli said. "We use a decoy."

"Who? Not one of my crew!"

"Certainly not. We use Anderson. He prospected out here and knows the ropes. We put him down in a prospect hole, furnish him with an electronic fence, a communicator and an automatic rifle and await developments."

"Does he know what you're planning for him?" I asked.

"Naturally. I hired him on contract for this job."

"But that's sending a man out to be murdered!"

"He did it before, with less hope of reward."

"But—" I shrugged and shut up. Anderson knew what he was doing—what chances he took.

"The greatest concentration of Corens, so I understand, is in the South Polar Region," Martinelli said. "We'll land near there and break out one of the lifeboats. Anderson'll set out and find some Corens. He'll land about a day's march away and set up camp, using the lifeboat as a base, and when the Corens come he'll invite attack, record their war cry, and then come back here in the lifeboat. It's simple."

Yeah—simple. But Martinelli didn't know the Corens. He had no experience with their uncanny ability to camouflage themselves to look like natural rocks or siliceous vegetation. He didn't know their incredible ferocity or tenacity of life, or their equally incredible patience. Probably Anderson did, but the man was hardly more intelligent than a Coren. It would be all too easy for him to become a second casualty, and I wanted no more. One death on this voyage was enough. As captain, I was responsible for both crew and passengers and I had no desire to explain to an Admiralty Court why I allowed a passenger to expose himself to possible death. Actually, I couldn't stop him. Once on a planet my authority over passengers was nil, but I'd be the target of some pretty hard questioning if anything happened.

"We're going to tape this insane idea of yours into the ship's log," I said. "I want it on record that I'm opposed to this sort of thing and that it is your responsibility."

Martinelli shrugged. "As you wish," he said indifferently. "I'll have Anderson make a statement, too."

I sighed.

ANDERSON took off in the lifeboat shortly after we landed and completed the usual security precautions. After searing a hundred-yard wide area around the base of the ship with the rockets on idling, we strung an electronic fence and hooked it to one of the auxiliary generators. The gun turrets were opened and our heavy weapons were checked to see that they were in operating condition.

After that, two groups of crewmen covered every square foot of the seared area blasting any suspicious bump or bulge on the ground. Then, and only then, did we break out a lifeboat, provision and equip it, and send Anderson on his way. As he disappeared southward, I had the feeling we would never see him again.

Half an hour later he reported in over the communicator. "Spotted about two hundred of the jellies—am circling them. Get a position fix."

Wagner, our astrogator, obligingly pinpointed him and gave him the data on his position.

"Will now fly about thirty miles away and find a landing site," Anderson said.

"Some navigator," Wagner said. "He doesn't even know his position." He flipped the transmitted switch. *"Queen* to Anderson. Will track you. Fly over your landing area until I pinpoint you."

"Okay, *Queen*." The transmitter stayed on as Anderson circled.

"You can set down now," Wagner said. "I have a fix."

"Thanks." Anderson's heavy voice was flat. "I'll contact you again as soon as I get my security up."

Regularly on the hour, Anderson reported. For the first 48-hour-period nothing happened. Then Anderson came on ahead of schedule.

"They're here!" Anderson's voice crackled over the phone. "I have about 20 new rocks in my front yard that weren't here yesterday. Looks like I'm going to have visitors." His voice was almost happy.

"Increase the charge on your fence," I ordered. "There's no sense in asking for trouble."

"I already have," Anderson said. "I know these jellies as well as you do."

"And keep your communicator open," I added. "You may not have an opportunity to open communication again. We'll stand by here."

"I'll do that—but there's no need to worry."

"Don't bet on that. The Corens are smart."

"Okay—but—" A wild eldritch cry came faintly over the communicator.

"Well—that's it," Anderson said calmly. "They've decided to pay me a call. I'll blast a couple of them to get things stirred up. Tell Martinelli he'll probably get his war cry any minute now."

"Was that a Coren war cry?" Martinelli asked. He was leaning over my shoulder listening to our conversation.

"No," I said. "But keep your ear glued to this speaker and you'll hear one. That was just their way of talking to one another. They have a tonal language, not an inflected one. They make sounds by forcing air from their air bladders through their breathing tubes. The principle is something like that of a horn. When you hear their war cry, you'll recognize it." I grinned thinly. "You can't help it. It sounds like a traffic jam of homicidal maniacs on the Mid-continent Skyway."

Martinelli chuckled nervously.

I turned to the ship's annunciator. "Now hear this," I ordered. "Prepare for blastoff."

"Why?" Martinelli asked.

"We may have to help Anderson," I said. "He just might not have firepower enough to get out of there."

Sound erupted from the communicator. It wasn't exactly discord, but it had a nerve grating quality that made the short hairs on the back of one's neck stand erect and icy prickles chase one another down one's spine. There were harsh undertones of menace, overtones of shrill hate, and a full-bodied middle range of detestation. I'd heard it before, but never so loud. It had the volume and some of the tonal quality of the brasses in an orchestra—a metallic diapason of rage and hatred. The sound swelled and throbbed inside the *Queen's* control room—and was suddenly punctuated by Anderson's horrified voice. "My God! There's thousands of them!"

"Get out of there!" I ordered. "That fence won't hold."

"I know," Anderson said, "they're all over the boat. They broke through the fence just like it wasn't there." His voice had become oddly calm. "I can't take off—they're weighting me down."

"Open the jets to full," I said. "Spin the ship. Shake them off!"

"I'll try—but you'd better get here quick. I don't think it'll work and this boat won't take much of that treatment."

"To hell with the boat," I said as I hit the emergency blastoff alarm. "It's your life I'm worried about."

"You're worried," Anderson said. "What do you think I am?"

Fifteen seconds later we were airborne—heading for the fix Wagner had taken on Anderson's position.

"If you can get here in another 20 minutes, I think I can hold out," Anderson's tight voice came over the communicator The background noises of his jets and the grinding of metal against rock indicated that he was taking my advice. "I don't dare try to roll the boat over, but the jets are scorching enough of them to keep the pressure off. The hull's bulging a bit but I think it'll hold."

"We're on the way," I said. "Hang on."

"I haven't any—" the communicator went dead. One of the Corens had probably ripped off the antenna.

WE flashed across Titan's surface, travelling low and fast, I don't know how the crew felt, but I wanted to get to Anderson while he was still alive. The Corens were incredibly strong, and a lifeboat isn't too ruggedly built. All they had to do was spring one plate and Anderson was dead.

"He's just over that next range of hills, skipper," Wagner's voice came into my earphones.

I threw the *Queen* into a vertical attitude, balancing her on the jets as momentum carried us forward. It was a dangerous maneuver, but I needed the jet-blast. It was the best weapon we had. Sweat poured off me as I balanced the ship on her drives, using the jet to kill our speed as we swept over the hills and into the valley beyond.

The entire floor of the bowl-shaped valley was crawling with Corens. The lifeboat was covered with them. As they sensed the *Queen,* the gray blue blobs began splitting up and moving away with startling speed as they extruded limbs from their amorphous bodies and ran for safety. They had no desire to face a full-sized ship.

But those covering the lifeboat didn't run. They clung like limpets as we plowed stern first toward the seething mass of siliceous flesh, our tubes blasting fiery paths across the ground. Some of them died in the jet-blast as I set the *Queen* down heavily in what was an arrival rather than a landing. Shock raced through the ship, slamming passengers and crew against safety webs and shock couches. For a moment we teetered dangerously as I stabbed at the steering jets, trying to keep us upright. Below me the automatics in the three turrets that could be brought to bear began pouring low order solid and vibratory destruction into the Corens still covering the lifeboat while the fourth turret speeded the departure of those who were still within range in the valley.

The *Queen* shuddered and steadied in a vertical attitude as Bernstein, acting without orders, opened the engine room hatch and dropped to the ground followed by five men carrying flame-throwers. At the sight of this easier prey, the Corens swarming over Anderson's boat, dropped to the icy ground and came scuttling forward on their pseudo-legs, trumpeting their war cry as they ran.

Bernie and his men met them with a wall of flame that crisped the foremost dozen into cinders. But the others came on. There weren't so many now, only twenty or so, but a Coren is twice the physical match of any human, and if one of those beasts got to close quarters it would be curtains. I swore insanely as I watched Bernie through the scanners, cold sweat running down my face. He had no business risking his life out there. Nor did those other five fools. He let them come to pointblank range and fired again. I yelled hoarsely as the yellow flames enveloped the front rank of the nearest jellies, and yelled again as the others turned and fled. They had had enough. Fully two hundred of them were dead, and that price was too high even for their blood-soaked minds.

The lifeboat was apparently intact as Bernie and his party walked cautiously toward it, I noticed for the first time that the men he was leading were the Solar Union people—and whatever feelings I had for their actions on Pluto vanished in admiration of their courage here on Titan. It took guts of the highest order to face a charging Coren.

Bernie opened the emergency airlock on the lifeboat and slammed it shut again as a thick grayish blue pseudolimb extruded sluggishly from the opening. The closing steel sliced through the jelly-like mass, which dropped to the ground, extruded a half dozen pseudolimbs of its own and scuttled off across the gray landscape. I felt sick. We were too late. The Corens had managed to crack the lifeboat's hull.

We had a little trouble getting the Corens out of the boat without destroying the recording apparatus, but the exhaust fumes of a small gasoline engine finally did the trick. Oxygen breathers like ourselves, the Corens were equally susceptible to carbon monoxide.

We hooked them out of the interior, two three-foot pie-plates of gray-blue meat, with a humped central area that held dozens of flat razor-edged siliceous spicules.

"They look like jellyfish," Martinelli observed as we flopped the limp amorphous masses onto the icy rocks.

"Maybe they do to you," I said, "but to me they represent something else."

"What?"

"Vampires."

Martinelli's eyebrows rose, but they didn't stay that way. Two of the Solar Union men came out of the lifeboat carrying something horribly slashed and deflated that had once been Anderson. The knifelike silicon spicules had reduced his space armor to ribbons at every flexible joint, and inside the armor, a shrunken mass of bones and slashed skin was all that was left. Virtually all the soft tissues of his body had been absorbed. And the greatest horror of all was that there was no blood.

"They're fond of men," I said bitterly, nudging one of the dead masses with an armored foot. "We're a delicacy."

Martinelli's face turned a pale green, but he didn't get sick. Experience on Pluto had taught him to keep better control over his stomach.

"Load the boat," I ordered. "We can repair her on the way. There's no use staying here—and there's no use bringing Anderson," I added.

We buried him under a cairn of ice and melted it into a solid mass with our needle beams, while Martinelli went back to the ship with the sound tapes and his weak stomach, and the crew connected the hoist cables to rings welded in the lifeboat's hull.

It didn't make me any happier to know that this recording was also perfect. Two lives for two noises seemed a pretty high price. Nor was Martinelli joyful.

"At this rate," he said bitterly, "we'll be landing on Earth with half our personnel missing."

"I know," I said, "and there's worse to come."

I was thinking of the swampsucker. That thing is almost legendary in stories of the exploration of the Solar Union. Of all creatures dreamed up by an insane Nature in a moment of homicidal madness, the Venerian swampsucker is the worst. That animal fitted into no known category of solar life. It was even a stranger to its equally weird fellows on the Cloudy Planet. They, at least, had some similarity to Terran and Martian phylogeny. But not the swampsucker. It was a survivor of an older and fiercer age. I didn't relish the thought of meeting it.

"But let's look on the brighter side," Martinelli said, interrupting my unpleasant thoughts. "There's Ganymede, Io, Callisto, and Mars."

"I'll try to be happy about it," I replied.

He smiled without humor. "Sufficient unto the day is the evil thereof," he said.

CHAPTER FIVE

IO WAS our next stop. The run was made smoothly and without trouble. Oddly enough, the loss of Anderson didn't seem to disturb the ship as much as I expected. There's a difference between dying fighting and being crushed by an impersonal Nature. Anderson had known what his chances were. The fact that he had accepted them made his death easier to take. Why, I don't know.

The Kalliks—big, birdlike animals with downy jet plumage—thoroughly adapted to frigid, nearly airless Io, were an easy assignment. The human colony raised them by the thousands and harvested their feathers for insulation. Our best synthetics couldn't compare with them either in weight or efficiency. Light as thistledown, the black plumage was fireproof, heat transmitting, and cold proof. Each feather possessed the peculiar property of directional transfer of heat. Turn it one way and every local erg of ambient temperature could be channeled inward. Turn it the other and heat would be channeled outward. The Kallik feathers had long ago done away with complex and cumbersome refrigeration and heating units. They lined the double hulls of ships, furnished insulation and temperature control for spacesuits, heated and cooled every dome city in the System, and most of the better houses on Earth. As a trade item they were almost priceless and the demand far outstripped the supply. And, since the birds couldn't live away from Io, the moon had a corner on the System's temperature control business. Kalliks were easy to find, and in the hundreds of Kallik brooders dotting the area around the spaceport, it was easy to find nesting Kalliks. The Solar Union crew collected the necessary recordings inside of four hours—and Martinelli found several chitterings of the right tonal quality.

I was almost happy as we took on more chemical fuel and blasted off for Callisto and the whistlers. The whistler is a solitary beast with sufficient antisocial traits to make it a problem to figure out how the species reproduces itself. Their call, a peculiar double-toned ululating whistle, is one of the oddest sounds in the System. It makes the listener want to laugh hysterically—and early explorers often did—with occasional fatal results. The effect on Earthmen is bad enough that the uninitiated are required to wear earplugs.

We set down at the lone spaceport on Callisto, checked in with the Wildlife Conservation Division, who were all too happy to cooperate with us when they learned of our mission. One of the field agents turned out to be a sound bug and had made several recordings of the whistlers, which he was happy to give to the Solar Union men for use in the Natural History Archives.

"See," Martinelli said happily, "things are working out all right now."

I nodded, unconvinced. This was what I'd figured to be the easiest part of the journey. The life forms on Jupiter's moons were singularly friendly and inoffensive. I hadn't expected trouble here and I wasn't disappointed. We stayed only long enough to record our log, visit the officials at the station, and compute a course for Ganymede now on the opposite side of Jupiter.

I WAS glad to get off Callisto—the great, red bulk of Jupiter hanging overhead made me uneasy. I always have the feeling that the Big Boy's satellites are falling into that hell of methane storms raging on the surface. It's not a particularly secure feeling since it leaves me with the same sort of vertigo that grips some people who peer over the edge of earth's skyscrapers. Aboard ship it's different, but on a planetary surface I don't like feeling like a cliffhanger.

We met Ganymede about ten hours out, overtook her and made the third landing in as many days. This business of satellite jumping was almost pleasant after the long runs from Pluto and Saturn.

"So you want to record the song of a Hegemon?" the Port Captain asked. He eyed us with amusement—one of those trim, darkly efficient young men who are taking over the Space Service. His voice soothed my jangled Norse nerves like a buzz saw cutting through a steel plate. I've never cared for Civil Servants who eye spacemen with amusement. We may be anachronisms, but we've done more to make the Solar Union work than a regiment of these neatly polished products of the Academy. "I'm afraid you're in for a disappointment, gentlemen," the Port Captain continued. "There probably isn't a hegemon on this world that would sing for you. We humans aren't liked too well."

Small wonder, I thought. If this character is representative of the Earthmen on Ganymede, the hegemons would probably be only too happy to see our retreating backsides rather than our faces. I glowered at the captain who returned the glare.

"Have you ever tried cooperating with them?" I asked.

"Why? We have no need for them—and they will have none for us. We leave each other alone."

"Oh—great!" I exploded.

"Easy, skipper," Martinelli said. "There's no need to antagonize him."

"Why not? The poor fool obviously knows nothing about Ganymede."

The Port Captain stiffened. Dislike flashed from his brown eyes to my blue ones, and was returned with interest. "Since you are obviously an authority on Ganymedan life,

Captain Lundfors," he said, "I would appreciate your views on the matter. They might help us."

"They might at that," I said.

"And what would you suggest?" he asked icily.

"Skipper!" Martinelli said, pleadingly.

I ignored him. "What is your job here?" I asked the Captain.

"To speed the work of the spaceport and improve efficiency, of course."

"Why?"

"So trade can move freely."

"What sort of trade?"

"Machinery, textiles, food, and living equipment from Earth—industrial bort, gem stones, and isotopes from here."

"No wonder the hegemons dislike you!" I said.

"Eh?"

"Do you know what you're doing?"

"Certainly—we're helping to keep the Solar Union's economy in balance."

"And you're taking without giving. Sure, I'll admit most of the stuff you're using is valueless to the hegemons, and they're perfectly content to let you have it, but after all, it's their property—a part of their world and you take without asking—and conduct a closed trade system—leaving them out. They're intelligent and sensitive in the mass, and they obviously resent being treated like country cousins."

"We have nothing they want," the captain said. "They're the most completely self-sufficient form of life in the Union. We've thought of a thousand things to trade, but they neither want them or need them. We've been on this world officially for the past ten years, and the traders and prospectors were here nearly a hundred more. No one, except for one man, has in all that time even roused the slightest interest in a hegemon. They tolerate us, but they've never shown any interest in our activities except when we built this spaceport and trading station."

"For trade between Earth and her colonists," I added.

"For Solar Union trade," he corrected.

I GRINNED at him. "I was here in '08," I said. "One of the Old Timers had hegemons doing his work for him. He shipped out with us with over ten million credits in his account."

"You knew Isaac Miller?" the Captain asked. There was a faint note of respect in his voice.

"Sure," I said. "That's the man I was talking about. What about him?"

"He was the only one who ever could work with the hegemons."

"Well—why don't you do what he did?"

"What *did* he do?"

"What? Don't you know? Why—he told me he was going to turn his secret over to your people."

The Port Captain nodded. "He was," he said, "but he was killed in a groundcar accident less than a week after he returned to Earth. And he left no records."

"Oh—I didn't know."

"And you know Isaac's secret."

"I think so."

"And you'll give it to us?"

"Why?" I asked.

"What's this!" Martinelli broke in.

"Remember me telling you that we'd have no trouble with the hegemons?" I asked.

He nodded. "But you were wrong."

I shook my head. "I don't think so. It's just that these Solar Union lads don't use their heads. They've been ignoring the natives."

"And what's wrong with that?" the Port Captain asked. "Just how do you trade with an entity that has no need for goods—which draws its sustenance out of the rocks—and who has such a completely different standard of behavior that it cannot even recognize that you're intelligent except when you're working in a group? The hegemons neither need nor want goods or money, and since they have neither sex nor sight, nor the ability to taste or smell, there's virtually no way to contact them. The things that appeal to us do not appeal to them. We have no common basics, no meeting grounds. So we go our way and they go theirs. There's one just outside the port—probably a million-unit cluster. It's been there ever since we phased in, and it ignores us. Once in awhile it shows a color change, but not often. It just sits there! For ten years it's been sitting there ignoring us. We've tried everything." The captain's young voice sounded human and a little desperate. "And nothing works. Why it stays around is a mystery. Maybe it likes to observe us—with whatever it uses in place of vision."

"No," I said, "it's hoping. That's why it stays."

"Hoping for what?" he asked.

"Hoping that you'll some day get some sense and give it what it wants."

"And what do we have that it could possibly want?"

"Music," I said.

"Music?" his voice was incredulous. "What would a thing like that want with music?"

"Possibly the same thing we do—emotional satisfaction."

"This I'll believe when I see it," the Port Captain said.

"Well, come along and learn something. We old-timers aren't quite as stupid as you youngsters think."

He didn't laugh, but his smile was condescending, like that an indulgent father gives a child. It made me writhe. "I'll come," he said. "I wouldn't miss this for worlds. We've tried sound on it. We know it's sensitive to vibrations, but it never displayed the slightest interest."

"Why should it?" I asked. "Let's suppose you were a music lover and someone kept jarring your ears with an oscillator. Would you pay him any attention?"

The Port Captain grinned. "I guess not—except maybe to hit him over the head if he annoyed me too much."

"Now consider the patience and forbearance of the hegemon."

"Hmm—I see—but we did try music. Arlo Jelke brought out a whole album of dance music—progressive squirm. He didn't get a nibble.

"Why should he? The hegemon is logical and rational. It wouldn't go for that stuff."

"Maybe you're right," the Port Captain said grudgingly, "but until you prove it I'm not buying."

We wore armor, of course. Not to protect us against the lack of air because there was plenty of that, but to keep the bitter cold from freezing us solid.

THE hegemon, an enormous one, was nestled against the base of one of the low hills just outside the Spaceport Dome. It was an impressive sight, gleaming a rosy pink in the red light of Jupiter hanging above us. A tremendous structure of hexahedral crystals, it spread over nearly half an acre of Ganymede's barren terrain, and as we watched, it moved sluggishly, rearranging the individual crystals of its mass into odd shapes and angularities and geometric patterns of startling beauty, I plucked a crystal from the branch of a surrealist tree that towered beside us. The tiny living entity scarcely two centimeters long, a perfect hexahedron with fine tendrils protruding from either end, was one of the millions of units that composed this monstrous structure of crystalline life. It glowed, first pink and then an angry red, as its life substance realized that it was separated from its fellows. Individually it was nothing—merely a unit in the mass—but collectively a hegemon was a thing of incalculable strength and power. The energies contained in this giant could devastate half of Ganymede if they were released all at once.

I looked at the crystal curiously and replaced it in the mass. Instantly its tendrils entwined with the others and its crystal shape blended into the growth around us.

The Port Captain looked at me with horror in his eyes. "You were lucky," he said. "I've seen men incinerated for meddling with a hegemon."

"Not for one crystal," I said. "It's too small compared to the total mass. But a dozen of them could burn your hand off." I turned to the Solar Union men who were setting up the recording apparatus from the ship. "You about ready, boys?" I asked.

Their chief, a grizzled veteran named Vance M'bonga, nodded—his white teeth gleaming in the darkness of his face. "Ready, skipper," he said.

"Did you bring that *Nine Worlds* tape?" I asked Martinelli.

"I did—but can't we use something else?"

"We could, but it would have to be something this fellow hasn't experienced, and I don't know whether this is one of old Isaac's boys. It's big enough to be, and the fact that it's been hanging around here for ten years makes me think it might have had some close contacts with humanity. So why take chances. We won't miss with this one—and I'd like to show that young fellow something." I jerked my thumb at the Port Captain. "Besides, I figure that patience like this hegemon has shown should be rewarded."

"All right, but I hope you're not barking at the moon," Martinelli threaded the tape on the stereo player and Vance turned the volume on full.

"There's always that chance," I said as I looked past him at Vance. "Okay—let her go," I said, "loud and clear."

The opening bars of Raposnikov's *Nine Worlds Symphony* crashed from the speakers.

Instantly the vast mass of the hegemon rippled. Its crystals tinkled like fairy bells, turned a deep red, and shifted with a dazzling rapidity. Before we could move we were encased in a throbbing mass of pulsating ruby crystals that soared over us and around us to form a gigantic million faceted, acoustically perfect dome that changed shades of color to match each change in tempo of the music. Two hundred of Earth's best musicians had poured their talents onto that tape and two million units of an utterly alien life form absorbed that sound with an intensity no human audience could match. Bursts of scintillating colors flashed and rippled over the crystalline mass around us, and the mass itself moved and rippled, approaching the stereo to catch the fainter parts, retreating from the full-throated crescendos, quivering to the glissades, and swaying with the rhythms of the melody. We were standing in the middle of a fantastic concert hall, a hall that lived with the music that filled it—that drank in greedily every note, every nuance of the contrapuntal passages, every chord and harmony.

The Port Captain, the sound specialists from the Solar Union, Martinelli and myself were stunned. I hadn't expected such a response even though I had known in a rough sort of way what would happen. The others, utterly unprepared, were struck dumb by the glittering fairyland that encased them.

Finally it was over. The last notes died, and slowly, reluctantly; the hegemon withdrew to form a gigantic mass, a tower of piled crystals that pulsed with ruby color. And from the glowing crystals came a pure clean note of music, so sweet and piercing that our bodies shook to its vibration.

"Record!" I snapped.

Vance moved, snapping the switch of the recorder as the note augmented, strengthened, and grew as the whole hegemon combined its millions of vibrating crystals into a wave of gratitude. We stood there, quivering, as the sound went through us and slowly faded into silence. The crystals nearest our feet drew back and before us, on the dark ground, lay a mass of black glittering crystals.

THE Port Captain took one stunned unbelieving look at the crystals and slowly sank to his knees. "Bort!" he gasped. "Industrial diamonds! Why, there must be fifty kilograms of them!"

"The audience," I said, "always pays for the concert. It appears that our music was appreciated."

"How much is that pile worth?" Martinelli asked.

"About two and a half million credits," I said, "figuring bort at ten credits a carat. That's Earthside prices of course. Your music has just shown its first profit."

"My God!" Martinelli's voice was as shaken as the Port Captain's.

"Of course," I continued, "there's the ship's share, the crew's share, the Union's share for taxes, and my share for showing you the secret. Figuring it out fairly, you'll come out about a half million ahead, which isn't too bad for fifteen minutes work."

"Look!" the Port Captain said. "The hegemon's breaking up."

Masses of red-tinged crystals, humming with power, were darting up and away from the central mass, which shrank visibly as we watched. Finally, the hegemon vanished.

"What does it mean?" the Captain asked.

"Simple," I said. "The word's going out. There's a new day coming to Ganymede. You won't find the hegemons ignoring you any more."

"I wonder if that's an unmixed blessing."

"You never can tell. Maybe—maybe not. And incidentally, Isaac said that they like Bach best, although most symphonic music will do well until they tire of it. Bach, however, seems to have the best lasting qualities."

"Thanks," the Port Captain said, "but it won't do me any good. By the time the word gets out everybody will be milking this golden cow."

"Of course they'll never pay like that again," I added, nodding at the heap of bort, "but a few classical tapes can be a profitable investment."

"But there isn't a classical tape in the whole port! We haven't a longhair in the station complement."

"Too bad," I said, "but maybe you and I can do business. I have a pretty fair library aboard the *Queen*. For twenty-five percent I'll let you have enough to make us both rich."

"You're a profiteer and a pirate," Martinelli said. "The only thing that gripes me is that I didn't bring any music besides the *Nine Worlds*, and I can't part with that. There's too much tied up in it."

"More than a few megacredits?" I asked.

He nodded.

"You can keep sole Ganymedan rights," I suggested, "as soon as you've produced the whole symphony. You can license it...or even work Ganymede yourself."

His face cleared. "Of course..." he said. "I'll license it for this planet."

We went back to the ship and negotiated a contract with the Port Captain who was happily contemplating retiring and becoming a prospector. I didn't tell him that he'd find it a lot harder than today's stint. After all, a hegemon that's waited for ten years would probably be more grateful than an ordinary native. And besides, it was probably paralyzed by the *Nine Worlds.* Its sense of values might have been distorted. But the young man would do all right—and I'd make a decent profit before Ganymede was glutted with music, and the hegemons raised their prices for helping humans make a profit.

CHAPTER SIX

WE braked down into a respectful orbit around Mars. The Red Planet was still the same suspicious place. Martians were never noted for their trusting nature, and with modern technology their distrust extended as far out as the orbit of Deimos. They had never forgotten how the exploration parties had nearly wrecked their culture with the exotic diseases the first humans had brought with them, and they were determined that such things would never happen again.

The Customs and Sanitation boat that came out to intercept us was filled with the typically fussbudget officials that have made Mars a trader's nightmare for the past two centuries. We were examined, poked, prodded, fluoroscoped, X-rayed, tracered, and decontaminated until we and the *Queen* were as sterile as an autoclaved forcep. And only then were we permitted to land. I couldn't blame the Martians. In their place I'd act the same way. We were too much alike in structure and metabolism for anything less. Human and Martian diseases flourished equally well in either race.

But this took time, and Martinelli was getting impatient. "We have less than six months left," he protested. "This stay in quarantine hasn't helped things any."

"It's the rule," I said. "It does no good to buck it. The whole thing is designed for mutual safety."

"But why do they have to move so slowly?"

"That's the Martian way."

"Ah, yes—the Martian Movement is called the *largo*. I wondered why."

"Your friend Raposnikov must have been a frustrated spaceman," I said.

"He could talk about the planets of the solar system for hours," Martinelli said, "and though he'd never been off Earth except for one tour of the System, he probably knew more about it than most men. He was a shrewd and careful observer."

"So it seems. Well, I hope he was right about his Martian sound effects. The thin air of Mars might make a difference."

"I'm sure he took that into consideration. He hasn't missed so far, has he?"

I shook my head.

We landed at Marsport—the domed Earth town on the outskirts of K'vasteh. Nobody paid us more than casual attention since spaceships were constantly leaving and taking off, and the *Queen* was neither large nor otherwise extraordinary. The Martians had been hearing the sound of jets for so many years that they were used to them, and the absence of the sound would have been more disturbing than its presence. We checked in at Customs, stated our business to a politely incredulous customs officer, drew our billet assignments and settled down to planet-side life.

The crew went off to stretch their muscles in the nearest bar. I sat in the port administrative offices cleaning up the inevitable paper work that goes with a Mars touchdown, and Martinelli went off to K'vasteh looking happier than I'd seen him in months. The closer he got to the sun, the lighter his spirits became. He was, I reflected, a true son of Mother Earth. The spacelanes and other worlds didn't interest him. His principal desire was to get through and get home to the familiar sensations of Earth. Mars, to him, was merely the third from the last stop in a trip that was already much too long. The temple bells at K'vasteh were just another sound that had to be obtained, and he intended to obtain them with the least possible trouble.

I COULD have told him something about those bells, but I didn't have a chance. He was gone before it occurred to me that he might not know. I learned about the Algunite monks a good many years before and the information was so much an integral part of my background that it was second nature. Algun was the nearest thing the Martians had to a Supreme Deity. When properly translated, the name means "infinite intelligence" and the bells are only rung for a candidate who succeeds in passing the examinations for the priesthood and on the annual Festival of Algun, which occurs in the summer on a date fixed by a complicated astronomical calculation performed by the Grand Ecclesiastical Council. Since the Martian year is over twice as long as ours, if we had missed the annual festival our only chance of hearing the bells would be to find a priestly candidate willing to take the examination and capable of passing it.

Finding a candidate would be no trouble, but finding one who would risk the examination was another matter. Since a suitable penalty was provided for failure, few acolytes were willing to take the examination, which was how the priests of Algun managed to keep a large number of acolytes to serve them. In my book priests were the only truly privileged class on Mars. Anything they wanted they had merely to ask and it was given them. The people, I suppose, figured that if the priests were on their side they could receive the benefits of infinite intelligence. And after all, there was some justice in the belief, because a priest *did* wield some awesome powers.

Oh yes—the penalty. It wouldn't be too much to an Earthman but a Martian's ears are much larger. A losing candidate lost his ears, and was driven from the temple. Most failures became hermits and hid their shame in the desert. The rest committed suicide. You see, a Martian's ears are not like ours. They're bigger, more brilliantly colored, and serve as a focusing device for psi-potential. Loss of his ears deprives a Martian of one of his six senses and impairs another. It was a high price for failure.

Martinelli came back looking downcast. "The spring Festival is three months away," he said, "and they won't ring the bells prior to that time."

"Unless a candidate passes the examination for the priesthood," I added.

"Candidate? Priesthood? What's this?"

I explained.

Martinelli's face lightened. "Then it's easy," he said with relief. "All we have to do is find a candidate who wants to be a priest—and make sure that he passes."

"Easy," I said without conviction. "Ha! Remember the ears?"

"What could be so hard about it?" Martinelli asked. "There shouldn't be anything we can't answer for him. We can surgically implant a two-way communicator and rig it into the Solar Union branch library here on a direct beam. With all that information to draw upon, a Martian couldn't help but pass *any* test."

I shook my head doubtfully. "The priests know every trick of cheating in the book. In fact, since most of them pass their examinations by some form of dishonesty, you might say that they are experienced experts in academic cheating."

"Do they know about micro-miniaturization?"

"I suppose so."

"But can you prove it!"

"No."

"Well, then—"

"If you can persuade an acolyte to go along with your scheme, I won't object," I said.

"Where would we find one?"

"Probably in one of the downtown bars in K'vasteh. They live it up during off-duty hours."

"Isn't that an odd sort of activity for a holy man?"

I shrugged. "Different worlds, different customs."

"Want to go with me and help find a volunteer?" he asked.

"Why not? The sooner we get this done, the sooner we get home, and the sooner I get paid."

Martinelli looked at me oddly—an enigmatic expression on his dark face. He nodded.

WE found our acolyte in the Garden of the Seven Delights, one of K'vasteh's plushier nightspots. From observation and experience I had long ago deduced that six of the seven delights involved alcohol, narcotics, audio, visual, olfactory, and sexual stimulation, but I never did discover what the seventh was. It involved something peculiarly Martian—about which the natives never talked. When asked they would respond with the irritating Martian cackle that can roughly be translated "find out for yourself if you're so curious." I'll admit I was curious but in a quarter of a century of riding the spacelanes, I had never found out. I figured it had something to do with their peculiar ears, but that was as far as I could go. And not having Martian ears, I would probably never learn anything more than I already knew.

Lor T'shonke was our lad's name, a Senior Acolyte of about fifteen years standing, a typical Martian, small, lean, pigeon-chested, and oddly human in conformation. Only his crest of feathers and scaly legs betrayed his avian ancestry. He reminded me of Commander Kelthorn's wry comment to the reporters after the first successful landing and return. "There's a bunch of queer birds on that world," Kelthorn had said—and the description was as good today as it was two centuries ago. Martians are queer birds.

T'shonke was in the middle of the First Delight—alcohol. A large amphora of Ko-fruit wine stood on the floor beside his booth and the peculiar narrow-mouthed sipping glass in his hand was half-empty. He looked at us fuzzily, his eyes half filmed by the translucent membranes of his third eyelids. He blinked at us, and I was somehow reminded of an earthly chicken. The lower lids of Martians are movable, while the uppers, encrusted in a mass of brilliant red pigmented tissue are more ornamental than useful. A Martian's eyes constantly give an Earthman the impression that all Martians are recovering from a three-day binge—but T'shonke was sober enough.

"Greetings, Earthmen, what brings you to this poor table?" he said.

Martinelli looked at me.

"Tell him," I said, "straight out. There's no ceremony. Just get the idea across fast and clean."

"How would you like to be a priest?" Martinelli asked.

T'shonke ran his long, bony fingers over the gorgeous ear, lobes that drooped in multicolored splendor from the sides of his head. "I would like to very much—but the penalty for failure is too great."

"And if we could fix it so failure was an impossibility?" Martinelli asked.

T'shonke's third eyelids snapped back and his yellow eyes were suddenly alert. "How?" he asked.

"Just a minute," Martinelli said. "What is your answer?"

"If you could guarantee that I would not fail," T'shonke said slowly, "I would pledge anything within reason."

Martinelli glanced at me.

"That's a top offer," I said. "You can go ahead."

"Would the contents of the Solar Union library be sufficient information for your purpose?"

"More than enough," T'shonke said, "except for the mysteries—and I'm well grounded there." His glass floated off the table, the amphora tipped, poured, and the glass floated back full. "I can handle up to fifty kilograms—which is twice as good as most priests can do."

"Amazing!" Martinelli said. "Are all of you Martians telekinetics?"

"No—just a certain percentage—like your telepaths—only better trained and better developed. We recognized ESP long before you did and made it part of our culture." He sighed. "If only our brains were designed for telepathy."

"That's where we can help," Martinelli said. "We can give you access to the Solar Union library even while you are taking the examination. In effect, you will be a telepath."

"How?"

"We surgically implant a fourth order communicator in your ear—back of the cochlea—and another behind your syrinx. This will allow you to talk to our agents in the library and they'll research any data you want. With the electronic coders in the library this can be done in seconds."

"They give five minutes for thinking," T'shonke mused.

"That would be plenty."

The Martian shook his head. "But it wouldn't work," he said. "It's been tried before." His eyes filmed over. "Two years ago an acolyte tried this technique. He was discovered. His ears are nailed to Algun's altar."

"Why was he discovered?"

"We go before Algun naked as we came into the world and are examined for evidence of cheating. Under X-ray the mechanisms showed."

"That's no problem—the communicator could be made of radio-transparent material."

"The size? Displacement of tissues?"

Martinelli held his fingers a centimeter apart. "That too large?" he asked.

T'shonke shook his head. "If you can do as you say," he said, "I will try to take—but wait—what do you gain from this?"

"The temple bells which will be rung in your honor," Martinelli said. "I wish to record their music."

"But can't you wait until the Festival?" T'shonke's voice was suddenly suspicious.

"You don't understand," Martinelli said, and then he told T'shonke about the *Nine Worlds Symphony*.

"Hmmm—I see. Now it makes sense. But before I agree, I must be sure that you are telling the truth. Can I hear this music?"

"Part of the first movement," I said. "Enough to give you an idea. No more."

T'shonke cackled. "You know Mars, eh, Earthman?"

I cackled back at him. "I do—a little," I said, "enough to know that Martians can't be trusted with non-copyrighted works of art, literature, or music. You're the biggest cultural thieves in the system."

"Not too much of an honor, considering the other inhabitants," T'shonke said easily.

"If you come to the ship," I said, "we can arrange an audition—a limited one—enough to give you an idea."

"That is acceptable," T'shonke agreed. "If I am convinced that the work of art is as great as you say, I will agree."

Martinelli shrugged. "But how will he know?" he asked me.

"I'd trust him," I said. "Mars has been a tremendous customer for classical music. I learned to appreciate it here. I had a month's layover between trips, and used to visit town pretty often. One of the Algun priests took a liking to me and educated my ears to appreciate great music. You can trust the musical judgment of a priest or most acolytes as much as you can trust anyone's. T'shonke'll give you an honest answer."

IT TOOK only half of the first movement to do it, I kept watching T'shonke and gave Martinelli the high sign as soon as the Martian was softened up.

"May I hear the rest?" T'shonke's voice was pleading. "It is the most magnificent music I have ever heard."

"You can hear it all—with the temple bells—the Corens— the hegemon—everything—once it's played in full and the copyright established," I said.

T'shonke's head drooped. "You are a cruel man, Captain Lundfors. You give one a sip of ecstasy and then hide the amphora; I could hate you if I did not know that you are right. There is no sense in jeopardizing such a valuable property. And so you are answered. I will help you. I could do no less—and though my ears may hang on Algun's holy altar, I will still help you. It will be recompense enough to know that I have done something for the greatest music I have ever heard."

"The priesthood should be some reward," Martinelli said.

"It is—but it alone is not enough to justify the, risk," T'shonke said. "I'm doing this for the music—the sixth delight—not for the honor and power of the priesthood."

I had never seen a Martian so moved. It amazed me. I had always thought of them as coldly intellectual and thoroughly sensual, but not emotional. Perhaps it took something as superlative as Raposnikov's music to move them and any lesser thing was not enough. Whatever it was, T'shonke was our Martian as much as though he had thumbprinted an oath of service.

It was no effort to install the tiny transmitter-receiver units and within half an hour T'shonke was connected to us by electronic bonds that worked perfectly well inside the temple and out. We tested the hookup thoroughly for nearly a week, under every conceivable situation. It worked perfectly, and finally, satisfied, Martinelli passed the word to T'shonke that everything was ready. We hadn't seen the Martian since that one night when we had recruited him but that wasn't necessary. Since we were in electronic contact personal visits were needless—and they would have done nothing to help matters. Acolytes who apply for examination for the priesthood are watched closely and suspiciously. T'shonke, we hoped, because of his long service, was not suspect enough to warrant being tailed prior to our meeting. Now, however, he was watched night and day.

We had already moved our recording equipment into an empty apartment opposite Temple Square and the Solar Union technicians were on watch day and night for the first sound of the bells.

And while we waited T'shonke entered the inner sanctum of the temple to take his examination. I passed the word and our whole complex linkage between T'shonke and the Solar Union Library in K'vasteh was alerted. We waited eagerly as the minutes dragged into hours. But there wasn't a sound over the hookup. Not once did T'shonke press the activator button. Night fell, and day brightened without a single call for help.

And then the bells rang out! A thunderous chorus pealing through the thin Martian air. From the two hundred-ton monster in the lower course to the tiny silver klingers in the uppermost tower, the great bell concourse rang out with a tone and brilliance unknown to the thick air of earth. And then, with a final shimmer of sound that slowly sank to silence, it stopped.

The cessation was so completely abrupt, so totally unexpected, that a thrill of fear shot through me. I had never heard the bells cease so abruptly before. There was something final about it, as though a period had been placed behind an interlude. Very much worried, I called the sound crew.

"We've got it. They're all on tape," Vance said with great excitement. "But all hell's popping down below us in the temple square!"

"What's the matter?"

"Seems like a lynching party. Gawd! They're tearing some poor native limb from limb!" Vance gasped.

I didn't need the letter that came half an hour later by messenger to tell me what had happened. "Honored Sir," it began. "I failed. The first time I tried the communicator and saw the High Priest smile I knew I was discovered. There was no doubt of it. And when I could not contact you, I knew, as neither you nor I did before, that Algun is truly Infinite Wisdom and His priests know about fourth order radiation. They took me immediately from the place of examination, cut my ears from my head, nailed them to the holy altar—and drove me from the temple. I am disgraced and maimed as no living Martian should ever be. The sixth and seventh delights are barred to me who enjoyed them more than all the rest. I now have no will to live, yet ere I die, I will perform one act for memory of the ultimate in music. I still have a set of keys to the temple. I know the stations of the guard. And for once the bells of Algun will ring for something greater than either priest or festival. Farewell." The letter was unsigned, but I didn't need the signature.

"What happened?" Martinelli asked.

Wordlessly I handed him the letter. He looked at it, puzzled. "I can't read Martian," he said.

I told him what T'shonke had done.

His reaction didn't surprise me. He looked sick. He loathed violence. "So we have the bells," he said in a dull voice. "Fine, now let's get going. We have only five months left."

"Four and a half," I corrected.

CHAPTER SEVEN

WE WERE standing on the shadow rim of Mercury. Behind us was darkness and bitter cold, and the lifeboard that had brought us here. Ahead was the blitzing corona of the sun and temperatures hot enough to melt lead. The sunward side of Mercury was an inferno, with soft crusts of semi-solid magma, spouting volcanoes and a ghastly brimstone atmosphere that corroded metal and ate through rubber and plastic as though the refractory substances were so much paper. It was no world for human beings, yet humans lived and worked here, extracting the heavy metals from the sizzling surface of the Sunward side and processing them for the use of the Solar Union's expanding economy. There were native life forms, the dominant one a grisly armored creature roughly resembling a lobster in size and shape. They were primarily vegetarian, and offered no trouble except for their numbers and the fact that they tended to congregate around Earth settlements or lumber painfully after exploring parties. Since they were neither good to look upon or to eat, men tolerated them as another unpleasant fact of existence on Mercury and tried their best to ignore them. There were about twenty of them following us, appearing abruptly from holes in the rugged surface, waving their long-jointed antennae solemnly as they scuttled over the rocky soil. Before us the flaming glory of the corona leaped and flickered above the knife black edge of the escarpment that separated us from the shimmering hell of the sunward zone. In many areas the transition from darkness to light was not nearly so abrupt, but we had selected this one because of the relative protection the escarpment offered. Ahead of us

Vance and his crew were pushing on toward the rimrock with the little remote controlled tracklayers that carried the sound equipment. In some respects this was an unnecessary journey since the sounds could be perfectly simulated by boiling a pot of thick gelatin over a low flame. But the contract specified actual sounds and so we had come to Mercury at the risk of life and limb to complete the next to last part of our mission.

Martinelli's voice came to me over my headset mixed with the roar and crackle of the solar wind as streams of electrons hurtled outward from the sun toward the farthest reaches of space. The static was inconceivable to anyone who hasn't experienced it, and here on the edge of the sunny side communication was virtually non-existent. Through the snap, crackle, pop and hiss, I managed to decipher Martinelli's words.

"Think," he said, "have gone—enough—up here and get out as—as possible. This place—on my nerves—"

"Me too," I said, and then repeated it a couple of times to make sure he got it. "Vance'll take the records—and then we'll blow."

"Good!"

Conversation was exhausting so we gave it up by mutual consent and watched the sound crew up ahead. They approached the edge gingerly and sent the equipment carriers ahead on their control lines. Electronic communication was hopeless up there. The tracklayers disappeared over the crest, guided by Vance and the four men of the crew crouched behind the rimrock with their recording instruments.

Time passed until Vance finally gave us the high sign and began to reel the tractors in. Two of the men, Tayler and O'Banion, packed up their equipment and moved back down the hill toward us while Vance and the fourth, a man named Stanley, his first *and* last name incidentally, brought the carriers back. The two recording techs were halfway down to us when the Merc-quake struck.

The ground beneath our feet shifted and rolled as we fought to keep our balance. The two techs were knocked off their feet and came rolling down the slope together with dust, rocks and boulders. The Mercurians following us scuttled back towards level ground, their antennae waving Wildly, I had the odd impression that they were communicating with each other, that their intelligence was greater than we thought—and then the whole scene dissolved into a kaleidoscope of chaos. I had the confused impression of a hundred things happening at once, that a giant rift had appeared in the wall of the escarpment into which tumbled the doll-like figures of Vance M'bonga and Stanley followed by the child's-toy shapes of the track layers, I was frightened beyond any fear I had ever experienced in my life.

I wanted to run—I *was* running, stumbling, staggering, staying erect by some miracle, leaping across cracks crisscrossing the tortured crust, dodging giant boulders and fumaroles that leaped hell hot and hissing from the torn earth. I was helpless and alone—more so than I had ever been in my life. The awesome power of the quake stunned and confused me—and it was nearly a minute before my reason took control and shook my fight or flight mechanism into some sort of sanity. Shivering with reaction and adrenaline I turned to face the direction from which I had come.

Behind me was shambles!

The quake had distorted the whole area, and through the dust and steam, landing across the rise to the cleft in the escarpment the intolerable glow of Sol's corona cut with brilliant light. Our lifeboat was miraculously intact.

Vance and Stanley were gone, but sprawled grotesquely on the torn and steaming rock were the two green-suited bodies of the sound crew, and bending over them was the yellow-suited figure of Martinelli.

"Hang on!" I yapped into my communicator. "I'm coming."

"Hurry!" Martinelli's voice came back over a roar of static. "Tayler's in bad shape!"

I CAME back almost as swiftly as I left. Tayler was still breathing, but he didn't look too good. A two-inch gash was ripped through the belly of his suit and there was red blood visible on the green armor. Martinelli was futilely trying to hold the gap closed with his armored hands and making a poor job of it. I tore open my emergency kit, pushed him aside, slapped a wet patch on the tear, turned Tayler's oxygen to full, flushed the suit, and turned to O'Banion. He was apparently all right—paralyzed with fear but otherwise unharmed. Martinelli was supporting him with one arm while the other cradled two flat canisters of sound tape that he had picked up from beside the men.

"You get it all on tape?" he asked as he shook O'Banion's shoulder. He wasn't gentle about it but he produced results. The man's eyes focused.

"Not the earthquake," he said.

"Merc-quake," I corrected absently as I arranged his companion to a more comfortable position. Tayler was breathing easier now but his face was contorted with pain. Mercury's corrosive atmosphere had cooked a large patch of his chest and shoulder, and he was suffering the indescribable agony of first-degree burns.

"I don't give a damn about the earthquake," Martinelli snapped. "Did you get those sounds of Mercury's boiling surface?"

O'Banion nodded. "They're in those cans," he said indicating the two canisters Martinelli held. "Vance sent us back with them. Said he thought they'd be safer—say— where is Vance? And Stanley?"

"Gone," Martinelli said. "They I fell into that crack in the escarpment." He gestured upward at the lance of light flashing through the torn rimrock.

"Oh gawd! Poor Vance."

"We'll have to get out of here," I said to Martinelli. "I'll carry Tayler and you take care of O'Banion."

"Why?" Martinelli asked.

"Because he needs help," I said. "And because I said so."

Olaf Martinelli looked at me with something like contempt in is brown eyes. "I don't need you to give me orders. After that fancy bit of running—"

"Sure—I was scared." I said. "I panicked—and I'm ashamed of it—but I'm still captain."

"Very well—captain." He made the title sound like obscenity.

I winced. It did me no good to reflect that I had come back. I shouldn't have run in the first place. A captain should never run—but the quake had done something to me that I hadn't realized was possible. It had made me afraid. All I wanted now was to get back into the familiar surroundings of the *Queen* and nurse my injured psyche.

But there was something else to do first. "You two get going," I said to Martinelli and O'Banion. "I'll be along later."

"Where are you going?"

"Up there." I gestured at the rimrock. "Mercury's gravity is lighter than Earth's. The fall may not have killed Vance and Stanley."

"What about Tayler? I can't carry him," Martinelli said.

"You won't have to. On second thought he may be safer here. Get back to the boat and try to contact the *Queen*. Have them send out a rescue party."

"But you're the only one who can pilot the lifeboat."

"Who said anything about piloting the boat," I snapped. "You can work the communicator as well as I can."

"But we don't dare stay here."

"We can dare anything until I find out whether Vance and Stanley are alive or not." I turned my back on Martinelli and moved up the slope toward the crack in the rimrock.

There is no point in recounting the difficulty of the climb, or the difficulty of the descent into the crack. I did it somehow and found the mangled body of Stanley quickly enough—but Vance was nowhere in sight. With frantic speed I checked the shattered rock, looking for something— anything—that would give me an indication of Vance's fate. I was about ready to give up when I saw a tiny spot of fluorescent orange gleaming from beneath a pile of rocks and debris. I clawed the covering away—and found Vance alive but unconscious. A rock had smashed his air intake, and in a few more moments he would be dead. I ripped my hoses loose and forced them into the helmet nozzle and gave him a stiff jolt of oxygen. Working as rapidly as I dared, I bent the crumpled intake back into an approximation of normal, connected his airlines, and dug him out of the debris.

He was horribly battered, but he would continue to live if he were gotten to medical attention quickly. Gently I lifted him, my big space-trained muscles easily supporting him under Mercury's low gravity, and picked my way back to where I had left Tayler. He was still there, but so was the *Queen's* second lifeboat. I was never so happy to see anyone as I was to see Egon Bernstein, and judging from the grin on his ugly face the feeling was mutual.

"Bernie," I said, "thank heavens you came!"

"Do you think I'd trust anyone else?" he replied.

I didn't say anything for a moment. Just stood and enjoyed the feeling of mutual trust and friendship that flowed between us. We'd been bucketing around the Solar System together for quite a few years and words weren't necessary.

"Get those two to the Mercury Station hospital," I said. "I'll take Martinelli back to the ship."

"How about Stanley?"

I shook my head. "He isn't very pretty. We can take care of him later."

Bernie nodded. "Well—there's worse places to die than on Mercury." He didn't say where and frankly I doubted if he knew a worse place, but he was a perennial optimist.

WE BLASTED off without Vance and Tayler. They would recover—modern medicine being what it was—but it would be weeks before either of them were fit to travel. We went back for Stanley, but the Mercurians had been there first—and I learned why they followed us around. Sooner or later, they hoped, I suppose, that something would happen to us. You see, they saw something in us that was important. Our skeletons were virtual treasure troves of calcium and phosphorous. And so they had *salvaged* Stanley. There was nothing left of him but meat. Every bone had been dissected from his body by the sharp chelae of the natives. The stories were right. Mercurians weren't carnivorous, but like all organic life, they needed minerals—particularly light minerals, and these weren't too common on the sun-world. We buried what was left of Stanley and erected a stone cairn over the spot.

CHAPTER EIGHT

Venus City was the same as ever—a dome town anchored near the north polar cap of the cloudy planet. Looking around me at the steaming swampland environment, I wondered how the old-time planetographers had ever come to the conclusion that Venus was lifeless. The formaldehyde and carbon dioxide in the upper atmosphere probably fooled them, as did the thermal layer a hundred kilometers up. But the ground level was just about like the old-time writers had predicted: hot, humid, and swampy. Venus was going through another Carboniferous period. Plants and animals of huge size covered the surface everywhere except the equator where it was too hot even for their adaptability. On Venus a high degree of specialization and relatively quick geologic changes probably explained why there was no intelligent life. The eras, periods, and epochs followed swiftly upon each other's heels and the geologic climatic and environmental changes were incredibly brief when compared to the other habitable worlds of the solar system. An epoch lasting scarcely a million years is insufficient time in which to develop intelligence, particularly when a million years on Venus were only two-thirds as long in duration as a similar period on Earth.

But there was life—plenty of it—and the biggest, deadliest and most indestructible form was the swampsucker. Imagine, if you can, a hundred-meter length of suction hose, two meters in diameter, armored with ten centimeter thick chitin plates, and possessing a rudimentary intelligence and highly developed sense organs that can detect disturbances in water pressure up to a half-kilometer away. Now endow that hose with a voracious appetite and a digestive system that can handle anything from leaves to animal protein and you have the swampsucker. Its toothless maw, fully a meter and a half in diameter, is ringed with hair-like stinging cells whose long processes, tipped with barbs containing a potent cytotoxin can reach out a full ten meters in any direction. Behind the mouth are two large collapsible muscular sacs set along the gullet. These can be dilated with extreme rapidity causing a vollent suction that engulfs any prey paralyzed by the stinging cells. Food and water are forced down the gullet and the excess water removed through a sieve-like valve in the stomach. The food remains to be digested, absorbed, and excreted through the long gut filling most of the posterior two-thirds of the animal. The nervous system consists of a series of ganglia connected by a doral nerve trunk. Each ganglion supports a number of sense organs roughly comparable to eyes and ears—and pressure receptors like those along the sides of earthly fishes. It is a formidable beast, that like the fabled Choggemugger, doesn't die all at once, and until men came to Venus was the undisputed lord and master of the entire planet. It isn't now. It had met a smarter, more voracious, more greedy life form and was rapidly being exterminated. If it only had brains it might have held its world, but ganglia are no match for a functioning cerebrum—and Venus was rapidly becoming man's world.

TO FIND a swampsucker and record its voice would take a full-fledged expedition, since the giant worm-like creatures had been driven from the polar and temperate regions to a thin strip of the subtropics girdling the planet where the temperature was too high for humans. Venerean life existed there in relative comfort, but even air conditioning and insulation couldn't make it comfortable for man.

It would require an expedition, which Martinelli reluctantly agreed to finance. It took a considerable amount of his share of the industrial diamonds to procure the necessary swampcats, men, and materiel. And since Venerean colonists are by nature dilatory and haggling, it took considerably more time. I didn't like this latter aspect since we had little better than two months to complete the contract and return to Earth, and time was running short. So I spent some of my own share of the bort to speed things along. At that, it took better than a week to accumulate the necessary gear—a task that could have been done on Earth or Mars in less than a day.

For some reason, Martinelli had become morose and unapproachable. He kept to himself and discouraged conversation and company. At best he hadn't been too gregarious. After nearly nine months in the close confinement of a spaceship, men normally get to know each other pretty well, but none of us really knew Martinelli. He was an island to himself, a closed system that none of us could enter. Not even I, who was closer to him than any other man on the *Queen,* could figure out precisely what made him operate. Lately he had taken to chumming with Bellini, the survivor of the two "experts" he had brought aboard, and pointedly ignored me.

I suppose I had it coming after that exhibition on Mercury—but why he should choose Bellini as a companion was beyond me. The fellow knew his way around Venus all right, but from an intellectual point of view he simply wasn't. He was a cultural cipher, his conversation limited to women and occasional monosyllabic grunts. The crew had milked him dry in less than four months, and while they tolerated him, they didn't exactly encourage his company. Possibly, I speculated wryly, it was a case of two misogynists getting together.

We set out in two swampcats—combination boats and tracklayers twenty meters long, armored and gunned heavily enough to discourage even the most ferocious life on this ferocious planet. A Venerean colonist named Riley, a big red bearded brute of a man, commanded one boat, and Bellini had charge of the other. And for the first time Martinelli didn't come with me. He went with Riley and I with Bellini. We kept to the waterways, watching the dank yellowish green vegetation slip by, and listening to the pounding rain that clattered intermittently—on our metal roof and the peaceful hum of the nuclear engine in its safety well amidships.

Five days found us well in the subtropic zone and the temperature was rapidly becoming uncomfortable. We pushed on more slowly—separated about two miles apart, twisting our way through the tortuous waterways, looking for swampsuckers. We saw one on the second day of our search, a young male, scarcely twenty meters long. The little fellow had guts if not good sense for he came at us with every intent of swallowing us, paused as he sensed that our size was somewhat larger than his own, and vanished in a pall of greasy black smoke as Bellini incinerated him with the semi-portable in the turret on the roof.

"They grow up," Bellini said coldly as he safetied the guns.

WE KEPT in close radio contact since we couldn't see each other, and continued to head southward. The ambient temperature rose steadily. Our Kallik feather insulation was set nearly at full negative. It kept the temperature bearable, but even so, it was miserable since the feathers did nothing about the humidity. Only Bellini seemed to be able to keep control of his temper. The remaining three of us, myself, Ward O'Banion—the Solar Union man—and Karl Albertini our native engineer, snapped and snarled at each other as the misty silence chewed at our nerves.

"We're getting into the area where the big ones hang out," Bellini said as our swampcat churned slowly through a weed-choked waterway. "They don't come into these shallows—can't push their weight through them—which is why we have the weeds. They need enough water to support them. But when we reach a clear channel—look out. There'll be one in the area."

We went forward slowly, partially on our tracks and partly on propellers, leaving a broad trail of dirty gray mud and torn vegetation behind us. The sunlight, filtered and diffused by the hazy atmosphere and the impenetrable cloud blanket overhead, turned the whole area into a misty nightmare where one direction was the same as another. A man outside would have no chance of finding his way back to Venus City. Even if he managed to avoid the deadly life in the swamps, the heat and humidity would quickly boil the life from him. It takes a trip to Equatorial Venus for one to realize how dependent man is on temperature and humidity. Our protective mechanisms of sweat glands and evaporation would be no help at all in this enormous steam bath.

I looked at the outside temperature indicator: a hundred and fifty—nearly at the boiling point of water on Venus. Farther south the water did boil—contributing clouds of steam to the hothouse effect that made Venus habitable only at the Polar regions. Men were at work terra-forming Venus. They had been at work for nearly two hundred years, but their labors had shown precious small result. The scientists figured that perhaps another century would see the breakpoint, when the carbon dioxide content of the atmosphere was reduced to the point where the hothouse cycle could be broken. Earth plants, bred for Venerean conditions, were doing their bit to absorb the excess gas in the air, and were doing it well—but the effects weren't apparent yet—nor would they be until the critical point was reached. The rains would come then. Enormous rains like those once seen on Earth in the days of her youth. And there would likely be floods—enormous floods that would put the stories of Noah's Ark to shame. And when it was all over, Venus would have a climate approximating that of Earth, and on the island continents rising above the shallow seas, Earthmen could live in relative comfort and build a new future. But that was centuries away and now men clung here rather than stood, and existed rather than lived.

I didn't like Venus. I hated its heat, its heavy oxygen-starved air, its swamps and insensately ferocious life. I would be happy when this trip was over and we were again in the clean blackness of space with the stars gleaming in unwinking splendor about us and the sun dazzling with its prominences and corona. And I would be more happy back on Earth with this Odyssey completed and Martinelli's fee in my pocket. A year was a long time to be on the flit, and like all sailors from time immemorial I would be glad to see the homeport again.

Our vehicle tipped forward into a broad scoured channel of black water.

"Here's a lair," Bellini said. "Check the ports and see if we're buttoned up. A sucker can get his stingers through an open port as easily as you can walk through a door. Check the ventilator screens, and see that every hole and opening is sealed."

I spread the word and the two crewmen and I checked the craft and satisfied ourselves that she was as tight as a spacer.

"All secure," I reported.

"Good!" Bellini said. "I'll start the oscillator now."

"Eh?"

"It's just an ordinary oscillator," Bellini explained. "The vibrating diaphragm is under water. We found out that it's the best gadget to attract them when we cleaned out the temperate zones." He flipped a switch and slowly turned the knob of the rheostat back and forth, listening intently as he did so.

I HEARD it almost as soon as he did. Or rather, I felt it. You don't hear most of the sounds an adult sucker makes. You feel them. They start in the subsonic range and rise to a ululating shriek that practically lifts the top off your head. O'Banion snapped on his recording apparatus and bent over his dials, fiddling with them for a moment until he got the mix right. He pushed back his headset and looked at me.

"Weird, isn't it?" he asked.

"It gets you," I admitted. And frankly I was understating. Subsonics depress me. Some people are terrified by them. Others become morbid, and still others can be shocked into unconsciousness. There are a whole range of responses that can be triggered by low frequency sound. Personally, I don't like them.

"Cut the engines," Bellini ordered. "Quiet. Don't move. Don't make a sound. There are two of them out there."

The whole vehicle was vibrating as two fat smooth waves came toward us from each end of the weedless channel. We crouched near the portholes watching the waves approach. From each of them came crimson glints as the dull light struck the upper edges of the giant mouth orifices.

"If those two are males," Bellini whispered, "you'll see something that you can tell your grandchildren. If one of them is a female, you'll see something you can't tell anyone." He chuckled, the sound a harsh whisper in the damp stillness that surrounded us.

Sweat broke out on my face as the two waves rushed together—and the water exploded!

A giant geyser erupted beside the boat and from the center of the boiling foam we could catch glimpses of the gargantuan snakelike armored bodies writhing and twisting beside us.

"Males!" Bellini said in a tone of satisfaction as the water boiled and heaved. An armored body crashed against the side of our vehicle, hurling us sideways through the water. The shock knocked me from my feet and as I scrambled to get up I saw Bellini slide into the gunner's seat and grasp the controls of the semi-portable in the turret on the roof.

"Don't!" I yelled, but Bellini was past hearing. His heavy features were convulsed with hate as he twisted the twin blasters to bear on the boiling water beside us. And the guns added their din to the roaring and bellowing outside.

Gouts of black smoke leaped from the nearest body mixed with puffs of steam as the bolts struck and incinerated whole sections of the monster. It was dead at the first blast, but its decentralized rudimentary nervous system didn't realize the fact. But it did realize we were present from the vibrations of our guns. A score of filaments leaped from the water and snapped around the turret as the severed mouth-parts of the monster attempted to seize and paralyze the half-inch armor plate of the turret.

Bellini twisted the gun controls, his face a mixture of rage and fear. Overloaded servos whined and a thin curl of smoke came from beneath the seat, and then the safety relays clicked as the overload became too great.

In that instant we were disarmed.

I LOOKED outside at the thick bundle of filaments and the ghastly nacreous pink of the two meter wide, roughly circular mouth orifice hanging from our topside, and as I watched, the filaments tightened convulsively as the front end of the monster died.

"Where's the other one?" I snapped at Bellini.

He looked past me. He hadn't heard a word I'd said. His eyes were fixed on the mass of protoplasm hanging from our topside. We were listing dangerously, our upper deck perilously near the muddy water as the weight of the front parts of the sucker dragged us down.

"Bellini!" I shouted, putting every ounce of authority I possessed into my voice.

He looked at me, his glazed eyes focusing slowly. "Yeah——what's the matter?" he said thickly. "What's going on?"

"You damned fool!" I raved. "What in hell were you trying to do—kill us? Where's the other sucker?"

"What other sucker?" His voice was thick with shock.

"The one you weren't shooting at—" I stopped. He wasn't getting it. Something had snapped inside his mind. For the moment, at least, he was merely an automaton. I clambered painfully to my feet. O'Banion was lying on the deck, bleeding from a gash over his temple. He was out cold. I looked down the engine room well. Albertini was sitting on the deck next to the reactor, his leg twisted oddly beneath him.

"You all right?" I asked.

"I think it's broken," Albertini said, gesturing at his leg. "I fell down the hatch when the sucker hit us. What happened up there?"

"Bellini blasted one of the suckers," I said. "Its front parts are wrapped around the turret. Bellini's in shock. O'Banion's knocked cold, and we're damn near capsized."

"That's no news," the engineer said, gesturing at the slanted deck beneath him. Point is—what are you going to do about it. We can't travel like this."

"First, maybe I'd better set your leg."

"That can wait. We'd better get straightened up and get out of here. Without guns we haven't a chance. You'll have to free that turret."

"Me and who else?" I asked. "I'm not going out there alone."

"Me," a voice said above me. I looked up. Bellini was standing in the hatchway. "I got us into this, and I'll get us out." His leathery face wore its usual normal stupid expression and his eyes were clear.

"What happened to the other sucker?" I asked.

"It's busy. It won't bother us. It's eating the one I killed. Oughta keep it busy for days." He grimaced. "Guess I sorta made a fool of myself up there, but I hate those critters. One of them ate my brother."

"Oh," I said. Actually there wasn't anything more to say. "Well—what do we do about the piece that's hanging on us?"

"We cut it off. Careful. Those stingers are still loaded. They'll stiffen anyone who touches them."

"What'll they do to a man?"

"I don't know. Nobody that's had anything to do with them ever came back to tell about it."

"Oh fine," I said. "You do the cutting. I'll hold."

He grinned at me. "We'll both cut," he said. "You may be skipper on the *Queen*, but you're crew here. This is my show."

I had to admit that he was right. We went back topside and I checked O'Banion. He was all right, but still dazed. In an hour or so he'd probably be as good as ever except for a headache.

CHAPTER NINE

WE TOOK brush axes, big broad-bladed things with razor edges, made for hacking through the tough rubbery growth on Venus' surface, and cautiously made our way out the after hatch to the slanting deck.

Filaments were everywhere, tipped with rows of fat, spindle-shaped excrescences armed with needle-like prongs.

"Stay away from those," Bellini said. "Chop 'em loose and rake 'em overboard. Once we get rid of those stingers we can start on the rest of the mess. He looked over the side at the gaping, corrugated, six-foot funnel of rubbery flesh. Dead, it was gray. Its nacreous red color had vanished, but it was, if possible, even more horrible than it had been alive. I looked down at the fringe of wrist-thick cilia surrounding its outer rim and shivered.

We worked slowly and carefully, cutting our way through the mass of interlacing filaments covering the deck, working slowly forward to the dense meshwork of pallid strands that virtually hid the turret.

"Damn! What a beast!" I muttered as my axe sliced through the rubbery flesh.

"You don't know the half of it," Bellini panted beside me as his axe sliced through two thick filaments. The gaping mouth below us sagged a little and the swampcat rolled sluggishly in the water. "Another four or five and I think we'll be able to clear the turret." He drove his axe into the nearest fiber.

"Yeah—looks like we're going to make it all right," I said.

"You never can tell—we just might be attracting another with all the noise we're making," Bellini said.

Involuntarily I turned to look up the waterway behind me, and the head of Bellini's axe whizzed through the spot where I'd been.

"What's the big idea?" I yelped.

"The idea is that Mr. Martinelli told me to get you out of the way," Bellini grunted. "And since you're no use to me now—" he swung the axe again.

I stumbled backward as the curved razor-edge split the air in front of me. I was numbed. I had expected almost anything except this. But the next time Bellini drew his axe back for a swing I was ready for him. I jabbed with the axe head, catching him in the chest. His feet slipped on the slimy deck and he slid backward into the nest of filaments still covering the turret. He screamed once as the stinging cells bit into his flesh and struck the deck as stiffly rigid as though someone had short-circuited his nervous system.

I felt for his pulse. His heart was still beating, so I dragged him back to the after deck. I felt like pushing him over the side, but there would be no profit in that. After all, he was the one who knew the way out of this swamp. I was no surface navigator.

Quickly I cut the remaining strands and dragged Bellini inside. Hardly had I fastened the hatch when the water boiled alongside us, and a great net of filaments shot out to enfold the severed end of the dead swampsucker as it floated low in the water. Bellini had been right after all. We had attracted another sucker.

Freed of the weight of the dead monster we drifted slowly toward shore, and once near an estuary that ran into the waterway, I started the engine and headed full speed into the shallow water. Behind us the main waterway boiled as a dozen filaments snapped out of the sullen surface to fall short by a good ten feet as we churned up the shallow waterway.

The big suckers couldn't follow us up here, and I wasn't afraid of the little ones.

I spent the next hour getting the engineer's leg bandaged, and a plastiform compress on O'Banion's aching head. Bellini was still alive and still rigid in a tetanic convulsion that left his limbs locked in extension. There was nothing I could do for him, so I went outside and cautiously removed the remnants of the sucker that were still clinging to the deck and checked the turret. It moved easily. Once again we were ready for trouble.

Then I checked the ship. The engines were all right, but the jolt the sucker had given us had damaged our radio. It was dead, and so was our main power supply. That collision had done more than cripple our crew. It had shorted out the main power leads from the generator and our entire electronic complex was a mess. Our inertial navigator was out, our computer was dead, and our radio direction finder was a hopeless mass of fused circuits.

"Think you can fix the electronics?" I asked O'Banion.

"I can try," he said grimly. "But I don't think so."

"Just what in hell happened to the relays?" I complained as I surveyed the wreckage.

"Someone wired across them," O'Banion said, as he pried into the breaker box. "Not a one of them had a chance to work."

"Why?" I demanded.

"This is Venus," Albertini said. "These gadgets are Earth-built and Earthers don't understand what we have up here. We work on hundred percent overload most of the time. We have to jump the relays. They turn our gear off when we need it most."

I didn't say anything, but I thought plenty. Here we were, three thousand kilometers from base in a crippled ship, hopelessly lost, and without communication. We could travel, but we were in a bad way.

"Well—go ahead," I said. "Meanwhile we'll sit here. It seems safe enough and it's going to be nightfall before long. There's no use getting worse lost than we are already."

TOWARDS morning Bellini began to stir, and by early afternoon was capable of some movement. O'Banion, however, couldn't fix the radio or anything else.

"About half the transistors are burned out," O'Banion said. "That jolt broke the primary leads loose and dropped them across the main bus bars from the generator. The circuitry's ruined."

"Oh great! How do we do without it?"

O'Banion shrugged. "Maybe we'd better ask Bellini. He should know how to get us out of here. Incidentally, what happened to him?"

"He slipped," I answered. "Slid into a couple of stingers."

"Hmm—sure made him stiff, didn't it?"

"It's lucky he wasn't killed. But I wish he'd come to. He's the only one of us with knowledge enough to get us out of here."

"Not the only one," Albertini interrupted. "I can do it too. It's easy."

"So?"

"Sure—all water on Venus flows from the poles toward the equator. Except for the polar mountains in the northern and southern hemispheres, the whole land's damn near flat. Down in the equatorial regions the water's literally boiled off as steam and the water from the polar condensation flows into refill what's boiled off. So you just pick a big waterway with a visible current and work upward against it. Ultimately it'll get you north again, and once we hit civilization it'll be easy to make a call into Venus City."

"Sounds easy," I said. "What's the catch?"

"Swamp suckers. The big waterways are full of them this far south."

"And how do we beat that? We haven't enough size or power to blast our way through a wall of sucker meat. Not if they're as big as those last two."

"They're not—at least I don't think they are," Albertini said. "And we'll have to take the chance. Otherwise we can run around in circles until our fuel deteriorates—and then we're done."

"Not a pleasant thought," O'Banion commented.

Funny, I mused, how different environments produce different responses. On Mercury, O'Banion funked out worse than I did, but here, in a situation just as bad, he was as cool as ice, I wondered what made the difference.

BELLINI never really became conscious the entire four weeks it took us to claw our way northward against the opposition of swampsuckers and other noxious forms of Venerean life that were smaller but no less deadly. He had moments of lucidity but quickly relapsed into the partial coma that had held him since the tetanic rigidity had worn off. He couldn't move and we took turns massaging his flaccid body to keep the circulation going and to prevent decubital ulcers. From what I saw, I doubted if Ivan Bellini would ever again be a useful member of society.

And as the days passed I became increasingly anxious. After two weeks I became frantic, after three, resigned, and when the fourth week arrived I lost hope. My contract was violated. By no stretch of the imagination could the *Queen* make it back to Earth in time for me to fulfill it. Time was up in another two weeks, and Martinelli would enforce the penalty clause for nonconformance.

I'd been suckered. Everything pointed to it. Martinelli wanted a free trip and a chance to enforce the penalty clause in our contract. At one stroke he could avoid payment and stand to collect a sizeable penalty fee. Yet, somehow, I didn't believe Bellini's story that Martinelli wanted me dead. It was out of character. You can't collect from a dead man, and I knew that my contract had the proper escape clauses. In the event of my death the *Queen,* if she survived, went to my family in Oregon. They'd sell her, of course, but Martinelli wouldn't be able to collect from my estate. Probably my crooked employer meant it literally when he told Bellini to get me out of the way and the dumb slob had interpreted him wrong.

No matter how it came out I was going to be taken. My passage money, the bort, and maybe the *Queen* herself would have to be sacrificed to satisfy Martinelli. As I thought it out a cold anger filled me. Martinelli might have me over a legal barrel, but I would have payment out of his hide if it took the rest of my life.

We ran into a swampland ranch about midway through the third day of the fourth week. The rancher, a leathery muscular character, superficially like Bellini, was glad to loan us a radio and a directional loop and give us directions how to reach Venus City. As quickly as I could I contacted the spaceport operator. "Get me Egon Bernstein, chief engineer of the *Virgin Queen* in dock at Bay 18."

"Sorry," the operator said.

"Sorry, hell! This is Lundfors—I'm skipper of that can."

"That's impossible," the spaceport said.

"So it's impossible. I'm still Captain Lundfors!" I yelled.

"And I'm still sorry, but I'm afraid I can't help you. You see the *Queen* filed a flight plan for Earth over two weeks ago. By now, she should be half way there."

"Without me?"

"I assumed you were aboard, sir. At least the flight plan was filed in your name."

I sighed—so I was marooned. I wondered how Martinelli had accomplished that trick. It was easy to see what he planned. He'd loaf across the ecliptic and arrive a day or so late—which would be enough for the penalty, but not enough to hurt his plans. I wondered how he'd gotten the crew to back him up—probably told them I was dead and gave them some smooth story that they swallowed like sugarcoated cascara. If I had been angry before, I was furious now. Martinelli would pay for this—and he'd pay plenty.

TO MY surprise, I found an account listed in my name at the Spaceport finance office. It held slightly over ten thousand credits and a note from Bernstein:

Martinelli says you're dead. None of us believe it, but time is running out and the Queen will have to be on Earth to finish her contract. Martinelli doesn't want to go—says it's your ship and until you're proven dead we have no right to take off. But I think he's trying to get out of the contract. So whether he wants to or not, he's coming aboard. He'll probably have plenty to say about what we're planning to do with him, so to keep the record straight and get us out of a bind with the law, here's your passage money on the next liner. With luck you should be waiting for us when we land. Sorry we can't wait, but you and I both know the ship comes first.

Bernie.

Good old Bernie! My thoughts jumped ahead. Without a licensed pilot aboard, Bernie wouldn't be able to land on Earth. Sure, he could call one up, but those things take time. It could be a couple of weeks before the *Queen* could get down if they arrived in a crowded period—and all periods were crowded on Earth. I had to get home quick.

I went down to the dispatcher's office. "Anything fast for Earth?" I asked.

"The Silver Streak", he said. "One of IPC's plush jobs with a two-week flight time."

"Good. I'll take a passage."

"Sorry—she's full up. But you can sign up and hope there's a no-show."

I grimaced, signed, and placed five hundred credits on the line to guarantee my passage. The dispatcher turned to deposit the cash to my passage credit and I took a quick look at the *Streak's* passenger list. One name struck my eye— Bellini—Ivan Bellini! He must have reserved passage before we went after the swampsucker. But he wouldn't be aboard. The sucker had seen to that. I was almost grateful to the beast.

CHAPTER TEN

TWO weeks later I was stretching my legs against the nearly forgotten gravity of Earth.

It didn't take me long to find that the *Queen* was still in orbit waiting for a pilot. She had three days left to fulfill her contract. It took me two of the three days to find a rocket jockey who'd take me upstairs and match orbits with the *Queen*, and another half day to persuade my friends around the port to advance me enough money to pay him. But I managed it finally, and half an hour after the jockey got his greedy little hands on the money I was entering the *Queen's* emergency airlock.

Bernie met me on the inside. "Skipper!" he said. "You made it!"

"Naturally," I replied. "After what you did, do you think I'd let you down!" I looked at him with that special look that says so much without saying anything. The same look he had given me on Mercury. "But we're not safe yet," I added. "We have less than seven hours to get downstairs. Now get cracking. We have work to do."

"Yes sir," Bernie said with a grin that nearly split his face.

"Oh, wait a second," I said as he turned toward the companionway.

He paused, half turned in the hatchway.

"Where's Martinelli?"

"Locked in his cabin. Should I let him out?"

I grinned thinly. "No, leave that to me. I'd like to see him again."

Bernie chuckled grimly. I suppose what I was thinking showed pretty plainly on my face.

Since we had a dock reserved, and I had a pilot's ticket for Earth's atmosphere, we received our clearance in quick time and I laid the *Queen* in dock at precisely 2345.15 hours, nearly fifteen minutes before the deadline. The contract had been completed on schedule, and Martinelli would have to pay up. But first he was going to pay in another fashion.

I made my way down to his cabin, unlocked it and dragged him out. He looked at me with goggle eyed surprise. "Lundfors! How did you get here? You're supposed to be on Venus."

I grinned and shook my head. "You're on Earth," I corrected. "On time. Now pay up—two million one hundred thirty thousand five hundred and twenty seven credits."

"I haven't got it," he said. "I'm broke." He laughed a flat bark that was nervous rather than amused, and I suppose he had a right to be nervous, since there's nothing lower in my book than a contractee who can't pay his bills when they come due.

I poked him in the ribs with a thick forefinger. "What do you mean? You weren't broke when we left."

"But I am now."

"You still have the symphony?"

He shrugged. "Of course, but what use is it? I can't produce it. Or don't you remember. Raposnikov's will gives it to me only if I can present it at the Decennial Celebration."

"So you produce the symphony."

"How?"

I shrugged. "I don't care how. You produce it, or I'll hang you up to dry. No court on Earth will deny my claim."

He nodded. "Admitted," he said, "but you can't squeeze blood out of—"

"A turnip," I finished. I eyed him appraisingly. It was a strain not to knock his teeth down his throat, and he wasn't helping matters any. But I held back the temptation and tried to remain sweetly reasonable. Since I held all the cards there was no sense in weakening my hand with a case of assault and battery.

"Why did you do it?" I asked. "What's the idea of trying to break your contract?"

"I told you. I'm broke, busted, penniless. I have no money."

"You had plenty when we started this trip."

"That was a year ago."

"What happened to it?"

"It's gone," he said. He grinned at me. That did it. I hit him then, a good solid smash to the mouth that dropped him to the deck and made my knuckles tingle pleasantly. I'd wanted to do that for better than a month, and the feeling was good. But it wasn't enough. Not nearly enough.

He picked himself off the deck and wiped the blood from his lips. "I suppose I had that coming," he said reasonably.

"There's more," I said. "That's just the beginning. That was for conning me. There's Nalton, Anderson, T'shonke, and Stanley not to mention Vance M'bonga and Tayler. You have a lot more coming to you."

He shrugged. "I suppose so," he said dully. The defiance was drained out of him. "But before you beat me to a pulp, I want you to know I'm sorry. I had no intention of killing or injuring anyone, and I had no intention of cheating you until I reached Venus. I did bribe Bellini to keep you out of the way until you defaulted on your contract, but that was only after I discovered that I was broke. I had radioed Earth for more funds and they told me that there weren't any. I had to make a decision, and knowing how you feel about money, I thought that if I could make you default on your contract, you'd be forced to wait until I presented the symphony. I wasn't going to cheat you. I intended to pay you once I had sold the *Nine Worlds'* copyright."

I laughed humorlessly. "I don't believe it," I said.

"That's your privilege. But you can believe this. Right now I'm not worth a cent. Without money to hire an orchestra I can do nothing. Unless I produce the music it's not mine, and if I use a public orchestra I will not receive more than a percentage of the copyright fees. So figure it out. If you want your money, you'll have to help me produce the symphony."

"I suppose you want me to give you a loan?" I asked sarcastically.

"Precisely. The diamonds you have will be plenty." He said this without batting an eyelash.

I COULDN'T help laughing. The sheer effrontery of the man was amusing. He was an artist all right. No one else would have the unmitigated gall to attempt to cheat a man and then try to borrow money from him. I shook my head. "Just what do you think I am?" I asked.

"Sensible, I hope," he said. "I also think you're a man who owes about two million credits to the spaceport authority."

"You're right there," I agreed.

"Then look at it reasonably. If you pay part of your debt with the money you have, you'll still be owing too much. You'll lose the *Queen* and with her your reason for existence. But if you take what you have left and back me you'll recoup everything."

I laughed at him.

"I'll give you a contract," Martinelli said desperately. "You can have all the profits if I can conduct the music."

"It wouldn't be legal," I said. "You could break a contract like that without half trying since it would obviously be given under duress. The money involved—"

"Money! Do you think I care about money? If you do you're an idiot!" Martinelli's voice was angry. "I can always get money. This means more to me than all the credits I can spend. I want the honor of conducting the greatest music ever written on its first public performance. I want to be worthy of the faith Nicolai Ilarionovitch Raposnikov had in me. He was my friend. He respected my skill as I honored his genius. He left his music to me because he knew I would treat it properly. Money! Bah! I spit on it!"

So help me he was telling the truth! I was certain of it. Truth has a ring peculiarly its own. Martinelli wanted to conduct that symphony more than anything else in existence. He wanted it badly enough to commit murder for it. I didn't believe his story about Bellini now. He was perfectly capable of arranging my death if he thought it meant that he would be the man on the podium when Raposnikov's score was played. But somehow that didn't matter now.

For the first time I recognized what drove him. He wanted immortality. He had sacrificed everything for this chance and before he ever could grasp it, it was being snatched away, I felt sorry for him.

"I can't understand why it happened," Martinelli said bitterly. "I shouldn't have failed. That money should have doubled. I looked the properties over carefully. They were as nearly certainties as any productions I've ever seen. I can't imagine how they could have gone wrong."

"Do you mean to tell me that you speculated with money earmarked to pay an account?" I asked in a shocked voice.

"It was a legitimate investment."

"In what?"

"Two shows and a musical comedy. They were good."

I groaned. It took a mind like Martinelli's to figure that angelling shows was an investment. "They flopped, I suppose," I said.

He nodded.

"You're the idiot," I said bitterly.

"At any rate, I'm a very, very poor businessman," he said. "Yet, I wouldn't have invested all my money if the cost of this trip had been less. Three or four hundred thousand would have made the difference. But since I didn't have it, I invested in the stage properties to make enough to cover your bill and the additional costs of producing the symphony itself." He looked at me and shrugged. "Now I can do neither."

It was my turn to feel bitter. I had been too greedy. We could have done the trip for less, but I was too interested in squeezing the last credit out of it. And so it appeared I'd lost it all. I shrugged. Actually I didn't have much choice about my future. Martinelli was the key to it. If he succeeded I prospered—and prospered greatly. If he failed I was finished. I had enough funds on hand to finance him, but not enough to pay the outstanding accounts, and this bill was too big to write off. There was only one thing to do—take Martinelli to a polygraph, and if he was telling the truth—well—I would like to hear the rest of the symphony with the sound effects we had collected. Men had died to get them, and they deserved something better than nameless graves. They deserved a monument, and Martinelli could give it to them.

"I'm a fool," I said. "I'm just about the biggest fool in the entire solar system, but if you're telling the truth I am going to finance you."

Martinelli looked at me incredulously, and behind him I had the odd impression that Raposnikov was standing there—smiling.

I'VE heard the *Nine Worlds Symphony* a good many times and in a good many places since its first appearance at the Decennial, but in my opinion there has never and will never be a rendition of it like the first. How do I know? Well— Martinelli and I have the only two tapes of that in existence and each time I play mine I hear something new. It's wonderful music. And it is complete compensation for the months of hell I went through to keep the *Queen* while Martinelli screamed, prodded, sneered, cajoled and bossed a hand-picked orchestra and sound effects group into the greatest performance that will be heard in this or any other century.

THE END

If you've enjoyed this book, you will not want to miss these terrific titles…

ARMCHAIR SCI-FI & HORROR DOUBLE NOVELS, $12.95 each

D-81   **THE LAST PLEA** by Robert Bloch
        THE STATUS CIVILIZATION by Robert Sheckley

D-82   **WOMAN FROM ANOTHER PLANET** by Frank Belknap Long
        HOMECALLING by Judith Merril

D-83   **WHEN TWO WORLDS MEET** by Robert Moore Williams
        THE MAN WHO HAD NO BRAINS by Jeff Sutton

D-84   **THE SPECTRE OF SUICIDE SWAMP** by E. K. Jarvis
        IT'S MAGIC, YOU DOPE! by Jack Sharkey

D-85   **THE STARSHIP FROM SIRIUS** by Rog Phillips
        FINAL WEAPON by Everett Cole

D-86   **TREASURE ON THUNDER MOON** by Edmond Hamilton
        TRAIL OF THE ASTROGAR by Henry Haase

D-87   **THE VENUS ENIGMA** by Joe Gibson
        THE WOMAN IN SKIN 13 by Paul W. Fairman

D-88   **THE MAD ROBOT** by William P. McGivern
        THE RUNNING MAN by J. Holly Hunter

D-89   **VENGEANCE OF KYVOR** by Randall Garrett
        AT THE EARTH'S CORE by Edgar Rice Burroughs

D-90   **DWELLERS OF THE DEEP** by Don Wilcox
        NIGHT OF THE LONG KNIVES by Fritz Leiber

ARMCHAIR SCIENCE FICTION CLASSICS, $12.95 each

C-28   **THE MAN FROM TOMORROW**
        by Stanton A. Coblentz

C-29   **THE GREEN MAN OF GRAYPEC**
        by Festus Pragnell

C-30   **THE SHAVER MYSTERY, Book Four**
        by Richard S. Shaver

ARMCHAIR MASTERS OF SCIENCE FICTION SERIES, $16.95 each

MS-7   **MASTERS OF SCIENCE FICTION AND FANTASY, Vol. Seven**
        Lester del Rey, "The Band Played On" and other tales

MS-8   **MASTERS OF SCIENCE FICTION, Vol. Eight**
        Milton Lesser, "'A' as in Android" and other tales

If you've enjoyed this book, you will not want to miss these terrific titles…

ARMCHAIR SCI-FI & HORROR DOUBLE NOVELS, $12.95 each

D-91   **THE TIME TRAP** by Henry Kuttner
        THE LUNAR LICHEN by Hal Clement

D-92   **SARGASSO OF LOST STARSHIPS** by Poul Anderson
        THE ICE QUEEN by Don Wilcox

D-93   **THE PRINCE OF SPACE** by Jack Williamson
        POWER by Harl Vincent

D-94   **PLANET OF NO RETURN** by Howard Browne
        THE ANNIHILATOR COMES by Ed Earl Repp

D-95   **THE SINISTER INVASION** by Edmond Hamilton
        OPERATION TERROR by Murray Leinster

D-96   **TRANSIENT** by Ward Moore
        THE WORLD-MOVER by George O. Smith

D-97   **FORTY DAYS HAS SEPTEMBER** by Milton Lesser
        THE DEVIL'S PLANET by David Wright O'Brien

D-98   **THE CYBERENE** by Rog Phillips
        BADGE OF INFAMY by Lester del Rey

D-99   **THE JUSTICE OF MARTIN BRAND** by Raymond A. Palmer
        BRING BACK MY BRAIN by Dwight V. Swain

D-100   **WIDE-OPEN PLANET** by L. Sprague de Camp
        AND THEN THE TOWN TOOK OFF by Richard Wilson

ARMCHAIR SCIENCE FICTION CLASSICS, $12.95 each

C-31   **THE GOLDEN GUARDSMEN**
        by S. J. Byrne

C-32   **ONE AGAINST THE MOON**
        by Donald A. Wollheim

C-33   **HIDDEN CITY**
        by Chester S. Geier

ARMCHAIR SCI-FI & HORROR GEMS SERIES, $12.95 each

G-9   **SCIENCE FICTION GEMS, Vol. Five**
        Clifford D. Simak and others

G-10   **HORROR GEMS, Vol. Five**
        E. Hoffman Price and others

If you've enjoyed this book, you will not want to miss these terrific titles…

ARMCHAIR SCI-FI & HORROR DOUBLE NOVELS, $12.95 each

D-101   **THE CONQUEST OF THE PLANETS** by John W. Campbell
            THE MAN WHO ANNEXED THE MOON by Bob Olsen

D-102   **WEAPON FROM THE STARS** by Rog Phillips
            THE EARTH WAR by Mack Reynolds

D-103   **THE ALIEN INTELLIGENCE** by Jack Williamson
            INTO THE FOURTH DIMENSION by Ray Cummings

D-104   **THE CRYSTAL PLANETOIDS** by Stanton A. Coblentz
            SURVIVORS FROM 9,000 B. C. by Robert Moore Williams

D-105   **THE TIME PROJECTOR** by David H. Keller, M.D. and David Lasser
            STRANGE COMPULSION by Philip Jose Farmer

D-106   **WHOM THE GODS WOULD SLAY** by Paul W. Fairman
            MEN IN THE WALLS by William Tenn

D-107   **LOCKED WORLDS** by Edmond Hamilton
            THE LAND THAT TIME FORGOT by Edgar Rice Burroughs

D-108   **STAY OUT OF SPACE** by Dwight V. Swain
            REBELS OF THE RED PLANET by Charles L. Fontenay

D-109   **THE METAMORPHS** by S. J. Byrne
            MICROCOSMIC BUCCANEERS by Harl Vincent

D-110   **YOU CAN'T ESCAPE FROM MARS** by E. K. Jarvis
            THE MAN WITH FIVE LIVES by David V. Reed

ARMCHAIR SCIENCE FICTION CLASSICS, $12.95 each

C-34   **30 DAY WONDER**
          by Richard Wilson

C-35   **G.O.G. 666**
          by John Taine

C-36   **RALPH 124C 41+**
          by Hugo Gernsback

ARMCHAIR SCI-FI & HORROR GEMS SERIES, $12.95 each

G-11   **SCIENCE FICTION GEMS, Vol. Six**
          Edmond Hamilton and others

G-12   **HORROR GEMS, Vol. Six**
          H. P. Lovecraft and others

If you've enjoyed this book, you will not want to miss these terrific titles…

ARMCHAIR SCI-FI & HORROR DOUBLE NOVELS, $12.95 each

D-111   **THE MOON ERA** by Jack Williamson
REVENGE OF THE ROBOTS by Howard Browne

D-112   **SON OF THE BLACK CHALICE** by Milton Lesser
SENTRY OF THE SKY by Evelyn E. Smith

D-113   **OUTPOST ON THE MOON** by Joslyn Maxwell
POTENTIAL ZERO by S. J. Byrne

D-114   **OUTPOST INFINITY** by Raymond F. Jones
THE WHITE INVADERS by Ray Cummings

D-115   **TIME TRAP** by Rog Phillips
THE COSMIC DESTROYER by Alexander Blade

D-116   **THE OTHER SIDE OF THE MOON** by Edmond Hamilton
SECRET INVASION by Walter Kubilius

D-117   **DANGER MOON** by Frederik Pohl
THE HIDDEN UNIVERSE by Ralph Milne Farley

D-118   **THE WAILING ASTEROID** by Murray Leinster
THE WORLD THAT COULDN'T BE by Clifford D. Simak

D-119   **THE WHISPERING GORILLA** by Don Wilcox
RETURN OF THE WHISPERING GORILLA by David V. Reed

D-120   **SPECIAL EFFECT** by J. F. Bone
WARLORD OF KOR by Terry Carr

ARMCHAIR SCIENCE FICTION CLASSICS, $12.95 each

C-37   **THE GREEN MAN RETURNS**
by Harold M. Sherman

C-38   **THE SHAVER MYSTERY, Book Five**
by Richard S, Shaver

C-39   **MARS CHILD**
by Cyril Judd

ARMCHAIR MASTERS OF SCIENCE FICTION SERIES, $16.95 each

MS-9   **MASTERS OF SCIENCE FICTION AND FANTASY, Vol. Nine**
Poul Anderson, "The Star Beast" and other tales

MS-10   **MASTERS OF SCIENCE FICTION, Vol. Ten**
Robert Moore Williams, "Time Tolls for Toro" and other tales

GOD, MACHINE—OR LISTENING POST FOR OUTSIDERS?

Horng sat opposite the tiny, fragile creature who held a microphone, its wires attached to an interpreting machine. He blinked his huge eyes slowly, his stiff mouth fumblingly forming words of a language his race had not used for thirty thousand years.

"Kor was…is…God…Knowledge." He had tried to convey this to the small creatures who had invaded his world, but they did not heed. Their ill-equipped brains were trying futilely to comprehend the ancient race memory of his people.

Now they would attempt further to discover the forbidden directives of Kor. Horng remembered, somewhere far back in the fossil layers of his thoughts, a warning. They must be stopped! If he had to, he would stamp out these creatures that were called "humans."

CAST OF CHARACTERS

RYNASON
His mental quest was leading him much too close to a very dangerous secret.

MANNING
Unfortunately, his ideas for colonizing that world didn't include survival for its native beings.

MALHOMME
This ruffian-preacher could be the one man that everyone might be forced to trust.

MARA
She wanted to save the aliens, but the big question was…did the aliens want to be saved?

HORNG
In the recesses of his brain was the key to a dead civilization—or a living menace…

KOR
Was it merely a legend, a king, a thing, or an insidious trap from another galaxy?

WARLORD OF KOR

By
TERRY CARR

ARMCHAIR FICTION
PO Box 4369, Medford, Oregon   97501-0168

*For more information about Armchair Books and products, visit our
website at…*

www.armchairfiction.com

Or email us at…

armchairfiction@yahoo.com

CHAPTER ONE

Lee Rynason sat forward on the faded red-stone seat, watching the stylus of the interpreter as the massive grey being in front of him spoke, its dry, leathery mouth slowly and stumblingly forming the words of a spoken language its race had not used for over thirty thousand years. The stylus made no sound in the thin air of Hirlaj as it passed over the plasticene notepaper; the only sounds in the ancient building were those of the alien's surprisingly high and thin voice coming at intervals and Rynason's own slightly labored breathing.

He did not listen to the alien's voice—by now he had heard it often enough so that it was merely irritating in its thin dryness, like old parchments being rubbed together. He watched the stylus as it jumped along sporadically: TEBRON MARL WAS OUR…PRIEST KING HERO. NOT PRIEST BUT ONE WHO KNEW… THAT IS PRIEST.

Rynason was a slender, sandy-haired man in his late twenties. A sharp scar from a knife cut left a line across his forehead over his right eyebrow. His eyes, perhaps brown, perhaps green—the light on Hirlaj was sometimes deceptive—were soft, but narrowed with an intent alertness. He raised the interpreter's mike and said, "How long ago?"

The stylus recorded the Earthman's question too, but Rynason did not watch it. He looked up at the bulk of the alien, watching for the slow closing of its eyes, so slow that it could not be called a blink, that would show it had understood the question. The interpreter could feed the question direct to the telepathic alien, but there was no guarantee that it would be understood.

The eyes, resting steadily on him, closed and opened and in a few moments came the Hirlaji's dry voice.

THE GREAT AGE WAS IN THE EIGHTEENTH GENERATION PAST…SEVEN THOUSAND YEARS AGO.

Rynason calculated quickly. Translating that to about 8200 Earth-standard years and subtracting, that would make it about the seventeenth century. About the time of the Restoration in England, when the western hemisphere of Earth was still being colonized. Eighteen generations ago on Hirlaj. He read the date into the mike for the stylus to record, and sat back and stretched.

They were sitting amid the ruins of a vast hall, grey dust covering the stone floor all around them. Dry, hard vegetation had crept in through cracks and breaks in the walls and fallen across the dusty interior shadows of the building. Occasionally a small, quick animal would dart from a dark wall across the floor to another shadow, its feet soundless in the dust.

Above Rynason the enormous arch of the Hirlaji dome loomed darkly against the deep cerulean blue of the sky. The lines of all Hirlaji architecture were deceptively simple, but Rynason had already found that if he tried to follow the curves and angles he would soon find his head swimming. There was a quality to these ancient buildings which was not quite understandable to a Terran mind, as though the old Hirlaji had built them on geometric principles just slightly at a tangent from those of Earth. The curve of the arch drew Rynason's eyes along its silhouette almost hypnotically. He caught himself, and shook his head, and turned again to the alien before him.

The creature's name, as well as it could be rendered in a Terran script, was Horng. The head of the alien was dark and hairless, leathery, weathered; the light wires of the interpreter trailed down and across the floor from where they were clamped to the deep indentations of the temples. Massive boney ridges circled the shadowed eyes set low on the head, directly above the wide mouth which always hung open while the Hirlaji breathed in long gulps of air. Two atrophied nostrils were situated on either side and slightly below the eyes. The neck was so thick and massive that it was practically nonexistent, blending the head with the shoulders and trunk, on which the dry skin stretched so thin that Rynason could see the solid bone of the chest wall. Two squat arms hung from the shoulders, terminating in four-digited hands on which two sets of blunt fingers were opposed; Horng kept moving them constantly, in what Rynason automatically interpreted as a nervous habit. The lower body was composed of two heavily-muscled legs jointed so that they could move either forward or backward, and the feet had four stubby but powerful toes radiating from the center. The Hirlaji wore a dark garment of something which looked like wood-fibre, hanging from the head and gathered together by a cord just below the chest-wall.

Rynason, since arriving on the planet three weeks before as one of a team of fifteen archaeological workers, had been interviewing Horng almost every day, but still he often found himself remembering only with difficulty that this was an intelligent being; Horng was so slow-moving and uncommunicative most of the time that he almost seemed like a mound of leather, like a pile of hides thrown together in a corner. But he was intelligent, and in his mind he held perhaps the entire history of his race.

Rynason lifted the interpreter-mike again. "Was Tebron Marl king of all Hirlaj?"

Horng's eyes slowly closed and opened. TEBRON MARL WAS RULER LEADER IN THE REGION OF MINES. HE UNITED ALL OF HIRLAJ AND WAS PRIEST RULER.

"How did he unite the planet?"

TEBRON LIVED AT THE END OF THE BARBARIC AGE. HE CONQUERED THE PLANET BY VIOLENCE AND DROVE THE ANCIENT PRIEST CASTE FROM THE TEMPLE.

"But the reign of Tebron Marl is remembered as an era of peace."

WHEN HE WAS PRIEST KING HE HELD THE PEACE. HE ENDED THE BARBARIC AGE.

Rynason suddenly sat forward, watching the stylus record these words. "Then it was Tebron who abolished war on Hirlaj?"

YES.

Rynason felt a thrill go through him. This was what they had all been searching for—the point in the history of Hirlaj when wars had ceased, when the Hirlaji had given themselves over to completely peaceful living. He knew already that the transition had been sharp and sudden. It was the last question mark in the sketchy history of Hirlaj which the survey team had compiled since its arrival—how had the Hirlaji managed so abruptly to establish and maintain an era of peace which had lasted unbroken to the present?

It was difficult even to think of these huge, slow-moving creatures as warriors…but warriors they had been, for thousands of their years, gradually building their culture and science until, apparently almost overnight, the wars had ceased. Since then the Hirlaji moved in their slow way through their world, growing more complacent with the passage of ancient generations, growing passive, and, eventually, decadent. Now there were only some two dozen of the race left alive.

They were telepathic, these leathery aliens, and behind those shadowed eyes they held the entire memories of their race. Experiences communicated telepathically through the centuries had formed a memory pool which each of the remaining Hirlaji shared. They could not, of course, integrate in their own minds all of that immense store of memories and understand it all clearly…but the memories were there.

It was at the same time a boon and a trial for Rynason and the rest of the survey team. They were trained archaeologists…as well schooled as possible on the worlds of this far-flung sector near the constantly outward-moving Edge, the limit of Terran expansion. Rynason could operate and if necessary repair the portable carbondaters of the team, he knew the fine points of excavation and restoration of artifacts and had studied so many types of alien anatomy that he could make at least an educated guess at the reconstruction of beings from fragmentary fossil-remains or incomplete skeletons … or exoskeletons.

But the situation on Hirlaj was one which had never before been encountered; here he was not dealing with a dead race's remains, but directly with members of that race. It was not a matter of sifting fragmentary evidence of science, crafts and customs, finding out what he could and piecing together a composite picture from the remains at hand, as they had done with the artifacts of the Outsiders, those unknown beings who had left the ruins of their outposts and colonies in six galaxies already explored and settled by the Earthmen; all he had to do here was ask the right questions and he would get his answers.

Sitting there under that massive dome, with the quiet-eyed alien before him, Rynason couldn't completely suppress a feeling of ridiculousness. The problem was that the Hirlaji could not be depended upon to be able to find a particular memory-series in their minds; the race memory was such a conglomeration that all they could do was strike randomly at memories until the correct area was touched, and then follow up from there. The result was usually irrelevant and unrelated information.

But he seemed to be getting somewhere now. Having spent three weeks with Horng, gradually learning a little about the ways of his alien mind, he had at last run across what might be the important turning-point in the history of Hirlaj.

Horng spoke, and Rynason turned to watch the stylus of the interpreter as it moved across the paper. TEBRON SPENT HIS YEARS BRINGING HIRLAJ TOGETHER. FIRST BY CONQUEST THEN BY... LEADERSHIP LAW. HE FORBADE...SCIENCES QUESTINGS EXPLORATIONS WHICH DREW HIRLAJ APART.

"What were these sciences?"

Horng closed and opened his eyes. MANY OF THEM ARE FORGOTTEN.

Rynason looked up at the alien, who sat quietly on a rough stone benchlike seat. "But your race doesn't forget."

THE MEMORIES ARE VERY FAR BACK AND ARE HARD TO FIND. THERE HAS BEEN NO EFFORT TO RETAIN CERTAIN MEMORIES.

"But you can remember these if you try?"

Horng's head dipped to one side, a characteristic movement which Rynason had not yet managed to interpret. The shadowed, wrinkled eyes closed slowly. THE MEMORIES ARE THERE. THEY ARE THE SCIENCES OF KOR. MANY OF THEM ARE WARLIKE SCIENCES.

"You've mentioned Kor before. Who was he?"

KOR WAS IS GOD KNOWLEDGE.

Rynason frowned. The interpreter automatically translated terms which had no reliable parallel in Terran by giving two or three related words, and usually the concept was fairly clear. Not quite so with this sentence.

"God and knowledge are two different words in our language," he said. "Can you explain your term more fully?"

Horng shifted heavily on his seat, his blunt fingers tapping each other. KOR WAS IS EXISTENCE WHICH WE WORSHIP OBEY ADMIRE FOLLOW. ALSO ESSENCE CONCEPT OF KNOWLEDGE SCIENCE QUESTING.

Rynason, watching the stylus, pursed his lips. "Mm," he said softly, and shrugged his shoulders. Kor was apparently some sort of god, but the interpreter didn't seem capable of translating the term precisely.

"What were the sciences of Kor?"

There was a silence as the stylus finished moving across the paper, and Rynason looked up at Horng. The alien's eyes were closed and he had stopped the constant motion of his leathery grey fingers; he sat immobile, like a giant statue, almost a part of the complex of the hall and the crumbling domed building. Rynason waited.

The silence remained for a long time in the dry air of the empty hall. Rynason saw from the corner of his eye one of the dark little scavengers darting out of a gaping window. He could almost hear, it seemed, the noise of the brawling, makeshift town the Earthmen had established a little less than a mile away from the Hirlaji ruins, where already the nomads and adventurers and drifters had erected a cluster of prefab metal buildings and were settling in.

"What were the sciences of Kor?" Rynason asked again, not wanting to think of the cheapness and dirt of the Earth outpost which huddled so near to the Hirlaji domes.

He felt Horng's quiet gaze, heavy with centuries, resting on him. THEY WERE ARE THOSE SCIENCES QUESTINGS WHICH KOR PROCLAIMED INFORMED WERE SACRED PART OF THE ESSENCE.

"Part of Kor?"

Horng's head dipped to one side. APPROXIMATELY.

"How is this known? Tebron broke the power of the priesthood, didn't he?"

TEBRON REPLACED THE PRIESTS. THE KNOWLEDGE WAS GIVEN TO TEBRON.

"Including the information that these sciences were prohibited?"

Horng shifted forward, like a massive block of stone wavering. His fingers moved briefly and then rested. THE MEMORIES ARE BURIED DEEPLY. TEBRON PROCLAIMED THIS PROHIBITION AFTER COMMUNICATING WITH KOR.

Rynason's head jerked up from the interpreter. "Tebron spoke with Kor?"

After a pause Horng's voice said, APPROXIMATELY. THERE WAS...COMMUNICATION RAPPORT. TEBRON WAS KING PRIEST.

"Then Tebron made this prohibition in the name of Kor. When did this occur?"

THE KNOWLEDGE PROHIBITION WAS COMMUNICATED TO HIRLAJ WHEN TEBRON ASSUMED POWER RIGHT.

"The same day?"

THE DAY AFTER. TEBRON COMMUNICATED WITH KOR IMMEDIATELY AFTER OUSTING REPLACING THE PRIESTS.

Rynason watched Horng's replies as they were recorded by the interpreter; he was frowning. So this dawn-era king was supposed to have spoken, perhaps telepathically, with the god of the Hirlaji. Could he have simply claimed to have done so in an effort to stabilize his own power? But the fact that this race was telepathic threw some doubt on that supposition.

"Are there memories of Tebron's conversation with Kor?" he asked.

Horng's eyes closed and opened in acknowledgement, and then abruptly the alien rose to his feet. He moved slowly past Rynason to the base of a long, sweeping flight of stairs which led upward toward the empty dome, trailing the wires of the interpreter. Rynason moved to unplug the wires, but Horng stopped at the base of the stairs, looking up along the curving ramp to where it ended in a blunt, weathered break two-thirds of the way up. Rubble lay below the break.

Rynason watched the grey being staring silently up those broken steps, and asked softly, "What are you doing?"

Horng, still gazing upward, dipped his head to one side. THERE IS NO PURPOSE. He turned and came slowly back to his stone seat.

Rynason grinned wryly. He was beginning to get used to such things from Horng, whose mind often seemed to run in non sequiturs. It was as though the alien's perceptions of the present were as jumbled as the welter of memories he held. Crazy old mound of leather.

But he was not crazy, of course; his mind simply ran in a way that was alien to the Earthmen. Rynason was beginning to learn to respect that alien way, if not to understand it.

"Are there memories of Tebron's conversation with Kor?" Rynason asked again.

TEBRON COMMUNICATED WITH KOR IMMEDIATELY AFTER OUSTING THE PRIESTS. IT OCCURRED IN THE TEMPLE.

"Are there memories of what was said?"

Horng sat silently, perhaps in thought. His reply didn't come for several minutes.

THE MEMORIES ARE BURIED DEEPLY.

"*Can you remember* the actual communication?"

Horng's head tilted to one side in a peculiarly strained fashion; Rynason could see a muscle jumping where the alien's neck blended with his torso. THE MEMORIES ARE BURIED SO DEEPLY. I CANNOT REACH THEM.

Rynason gazed pensively at the interpreter as these words were recorded. What could have happened during that conversation that would have caused its memory to be so deeply buried?

"Can you find among any of the rest of Tebron's memories any thoughts about Kor?"

YES. TEBRON HAD MEMORIES THAT HE HAD COMMUNICATED WITH KOR, BUT THESE ARE FLEETING. THERE IS NOTHING CLEAR.

The Hirlaji was shaking, his entire body trembling with some sort of tension which even communicated itself through the interpreter, causing the stylus to quaver and jump forward, dragging a jagged line across the paper. Rynason stared up at the alien, feeling a chill down his back which seemed to penetrate through to his chest and lungs. This massive creature was shaking like the rumbling warnings of an earthquake, his eyes cast downward from the deep shadows of their sockets; Rynason could almost feel the weight of their gaze like a heavy, dark blanket. He lifted the interpreter's mike slowly.

"Your race does not forget," he said softly. "Why can't you remember this conversation?"

Horng's four-digited hands clasped tightly and the powerful tendons stood out starkly on the heavy wrists as Horng drew in long breaths of air, the sound of his breathing loud in the great space under the dome.

THERE IS NOTHING CLEAR. THERE IS NOTHING CLEAR.

CHAPTER TWO

The Earthman called the town Hirlaj too, because the spaceport was there. It was a new town, only a few months old, but the gleaming alloys of the buildings were already coated with dirt and pitted by the frequent dust storms that swept through. Garbage littered the alleys; its odor was strange but still foul in the alien atmosphere. The small, darting creatures were here too, foraging in the alleys and the outskirts of the town, where the streets ended in garbage heaps and new cemeteries or faded into the trackless flat where the spacers touched down.

The Earthmen filled the streets … drinking, fighting, laughing and cursing, arguing over money or power or, sometimes, women. The women here were hard and self-sufficient, following the path of Terran expansion in the stars and taking what they felt was due them as women or what they could get as men. Supply houses did a thriving business, their prices high between shipments on the spacers from the inner worlds; bars and gambling houses stayed open all night; rooming houses and restaurants and laundries displayed crude handlettered signs along the streets.

Rynason pushed his way through a jostling crowd outside the door of a bar. He was supposed to meet the head of his Survey team here—Rice Manning, who had been pushing the survey as hard as he could since the day they'd set foot on Hirlaj. Manning was hard and ambitious—a leader of men, Rynason thought sardonically as he surveyed the tables in the dim interior. The floor of the bar was a dirty plastic-metal alloy, already scuffed and in places bloodstained. The tables were of the cheap, light metals so common on the spacer-supplied worlds of the Edge, and they wobbled.

The low-ceilinged room was crowded with men. Rynason didn't know many of them by name, but he recognized a lot of the faces. The men of the Edge, though they lacked money, education, often brains and usually ethics, at least had the quality of distinctiveness: they didn't fit the half-dozen convenient molds which the highly developed culture of the inner worlds fitted over the more civilized citizens of the Terran Federation. These men were too self-interested to follow the group-thoughts which controlled the centers of empire, and the seams and wrinkles of their faces stamped a rough kind of individuality even more visually upon them.

Of them all, the man who was instantly recognizable in any crowd like this was Rene Malhomme; Rynason immediately saw the man in one corner of the room. He stood six and a half feet tall, heavily muscled and a bit wild-eyed; his greying hair fell in disorder over his dirty forehead and sprayed out over his ears. He was surrounded by laughing and shouting men; Rynason couldn't tell from this distance whether he was engaged in one of his usual heated arguments on religion or in his other avocation of recounting stories of the women he had "converted". He waved a black-lettered sign saying REPENT! over his head—but then, he always did.

Rynason found Manning in the back, sitting under a cheap print of a Picasso nude with cold light trained on it in typically bad taste. He had a woman with him. Rynason recognized her—Mara Stephens, in charge of communications and supplies for the survey team. She was a strange girl, aloof but not hard, and she carried herself with a quiet dignity. What was she doing with Manning?

He passed a waiter on his way to the table and ordered a drink. Malhomme saw him as he passed: "Lee Rynason! Come and join me in repentance! Give your soul to God and your money to the barman, for as the prophet sayeth, lo, I am dry! Join us!"

Rynason grinned and shook his head, walking past. He grabbed one of the light-metal chairs and sat down next to Mara.

"You wanted to see me," he said to Manning.

Manning looked up at him to apparent surprise. "Lee! Yes, yes—sit down. Wait, we'll get you a drink."

So he was in that kind of a mood. "I've got one coming," Rynason said. "What's our problem today?"

Manning smiled broadly. "No problem, Lee; no problem at all. Not unless you want to make one." He chuckled goodnaturedly, a tacit statement that he was expecting no such thing. "I've got good news today, by god. You tell him, Mara."

Rynason turned to the girl, who smiled briefly. "It just came over the telecom," she said. "Manning has a good chance for the governorship here. The Council is supposed to announce its decision in two weeks."

Rynason looked over at Manning, his face expressionless. "Congratulations. How did this happen?"

"I've got an inside track; friend of mine knows several of the big guys. Throws parties, things like that. He's been putting in a word for me, here and there."

"Isn't this a bit out of your line?" Rynason said.

Manning sat back, a large man with close-cropped dark hair and heavy features. His beard was trimmed to a thin line along the ridge of his jaw—a style that was popular on the inner worlds, but rarely seen here on the Edge. "This *is* my line," he said. "God, this is what I was after when I took this damned job. Survey teams are a dime a dozen out here, Lee; it's no job for a man."

"We've got sort of a special case here," Rynason said evenly, glancing at Mara. She smiled at him. "We haven't run into any alien races before that were intelligent."

Manning laughed, and took a long swallow of his drink. "Twenty-six lousy horsefaces—now there's an important discovery for you. No, Lee, this is peanuts. For that matter, they may be running into intelligent aliens all over the Edge by now—communication isn't so reliable out here that we'd necessarily know about it. What we've found here isn't any more important than all the rubble and trash the Outsiders left behind."

"Still, it *is* unique so far," Mara said.

"I'll tell you exactly how unique it is," Manning said, leaning forward and setting down his glass with a bang. "It's just unique enough that I can make it sound important in my report to the Council. I can make myself sound a little impressive. That's how important it is; no more than that."

Rynason pursed his lips, but didn't say anything. The waiter arrived with his drink; he threw a green coin onto the table which was scooped up before it had finished ringing to a stop, and sat back with the glass in his hand.

"Is that your pitch to the Council?" he asked. "You're telling them that Hirlaj is an important archaeological area and that's why you should get the governorship?"

"Something like that," Manning nodded. "That, and my friend at Seventeenth Cluster headquarters. Incidentally, he's an idiot and a slob—turns on quadsense telemuse instead of working, drinks hopsbrau from his own sector.

I can't stand him. But I did him a few favors, just in case, and they're paying off."

"I think it's marvelous the way our frontier policy caters to the colonists," Mara said quietly. She was still smiling, but it was an ironic smile which suddenly struck Rynason as characteristic of her.

He knew exactly what she meant. Manning's little push for power was nothing new or shocking in Terran frontier politics. With the rapid expansion of the Edge through the centuries, the frontier policy of the Confederation had had to adapt itself to comparatively slipshod methods of setting up governments in the newly-opened areas. Back in the early days they'd tried sending out trained men from each Cluster headquarters, but that had been foredoomed to failure: travel between the stars was slow, and too often the governors had arrived after local officialdoms had already been established, and there had been clashes. The colonists had almost always backed the local governments, and there were a few full-scale revolts when the system had been backed too militantly by Cluster headquarters.

So the Local Autonomy System had been sanctioned. The colonists would always support their own men, who at least knew conditions in the areas they were to govern. But since this necessarily limited the choice of Edge governorships to the roustabouts and drifters who wandered the outworlds, the resulting administrations were probably even more corrupt than they had been under the old system of what had amounted to centralized graft. The Cluster Councils retained the power of appointing the local governors, but aside from that the newly-opened worlds of the Edge were completely under their own rule. Some of the more vocal critics of the Local Autonomy System had dubbed it instead the Indigenous Corruption System; it was by now a fairly standard nickname in the outworlds.

The system made for a wide-open frontier—bustling, wild, hectic, and rich. For the worlds of the Edge were untamed worlds, raw and forbidding, and the policy of the Councils was calculated to attract the kind of men who not only could but would open these frontiers. The roustabouts, the low drifters of the spaceways…men who were hard and strong from repeated knocks, who were looking for a way to work or fight their way up. The lean and hungry of the outworlds.

Rynason glanced across the table at Manning. He was neither lean nor hungry, but he had that look in his eyes. Rynason had been around the Edge for years—his father had travelled the spacers in the commercial lines—and he had seen that look on many men, in the fields and mines, in the spaceports, in the quickly-tarnished prefab towns that sprang up almost overnight when a planetfall was made. He could recognize it on Manning despite the man's casual, self-satisfied expression.

"You don't have to worry about the colonists here," Manning was saying to the girl. "I'll treat 'em decently. There'll be money to be made here, and I can make it without stepping on too many toes."

Mara seemed amused. "And what would happen if you *had* to step on them to make your money? What if Hirlaj doesn't turn out to have any natural resources worth exploiting—a whole civilization has been here for thousands of years? What if the colony here starts to falter, and the men move on?"

Manning frowned at her for a moment, then gave a grunting laugh. "No chance of that. It's like Lee was just saying—this planet is an important discovery—we've got tame aliens here, intelligent horsefaces that you can lead around with a rope on their necks. That alone will draw tourists. Maybe well set up an official Restricted Ground, a sort of reservation."

"A zoo, you mean," Rynason interrupted.

Manning raised an amused eyebrow at him. "A reservation, I said. You know what reservations are like, Lee."

Rynason glared at the heavier man, then subsided. There was no point in getting into a fight over if's and maybe's; in the outworlds you learned quickly to confine your clashes to tangibles. "Why did you want to see me?" he said.

"I want your preliminary report completed," Manning said. "I've got to have my complete report collated and transmitted within the week, if it's to have any effect on the Council. Most of the boys have got them in already; Breune and Larsborg have promised theirs within four days. But you're still holding me up."

Rynason took a long swallow of his drink and put it down empty. The noise and smell of the bar seemed to grow around him, washing over him. It might have been the effects of the tarpaq in the drink, but he felt his stomach tighten and turn slightly when he thought of how Earth's culture presented itself, warped itself, here on the frontier Edge. Was this land of mercenary, slipshod rush really what had carried Earthmen to the stars?

"I don't know if I'll have much to report for at least a week," he said shortly.

"Then give me a report on what you've got!" Manning snapped. "If nothing else, turn in your transcripts and I'll do the report myself; I can handle it. What the hell do you mean, you won't have much to report?"

"Larsborg said the same thing," Mara interjected.

"Larsborg said he'd have his report ready in a couple of days anyway!"

"I'll give you what I've got as soon as I can," Rynason said. "But things are just beginning to break for me—did you see my note this afternoon?"

"Yes, of course. The part about this Tedron or whatever his name was?"

"Tebron Marl. He's the link between their barbaric and civilized periods. I've only begun to get into it."

Manning was waving for more drinks; he caught a waiter's eye and then turned back to Rynason. "What's this nonsense about some damned block you ran into? Have you got a crazy horse on your hands?"

"There's something strange there," Rynason said. "He tells me this Tebron was actually supposed to have communicated with their god, or whatever he was. It sounds crazy, all right. But there's more to it than that, I'm sure of it. I wanted time to go into it further before I made my report."

"I think you've got a nut alien there, boy. Don't let him foul you up; you're one of my best men."

Rynason almost sneered, but he managed to bring it out as a grin. The role of protective father did not sit well on Manning's shoulders. "We're dealing here with a remarkably sane race," he pointed out. "The very fact that they have total recall argues against any insanity in them. There've been experiments on the inner worlds for over a century now, trying to bring out total recall in us, and not much luck so far. We're a sick, hung-up race."

Manning slapped his hand down on the table. "What the hell are you trying to do, Lee? Are you trying to measure these aliens by our standards? I thought you had

119

better sense. Total recall doesn't necessarily mean a damn thing in them—but when they start telling you straightforward and cold that they've talked with some god, and then they throw what sounds like an anxiety fit right in front of you… Well, what does it sound like to you?"

Rynason accepted one of the drinks that the waiter banged down on the table and took a sip. He felt lightheaded. "It would have been an anxiety fit if Horng had been human," he said. "But you're right, I do know better than to judge him by our standards. No, it was something else."

"What, then?"

He shook his head. "I don't know. That's the point—I can't give you a decent report until I find out."

"Then, dammit, give me an *indecent* report! Fill it out with some very learned speculations, you know the type…" Manning stopped, and grinned. "Speaking of indecent reports, what have we turned up on their sex lives?"

"Marc Stoworth covered that in his report yesterday," Mara said. "They're unisexual, and their sex life is singularly boring, if you'll pardon the expression. At least, Stoworth says so. If it weren't I'm sure he'd tell us all about it."

Manning chuckled. "Yes, I imagine you're right; Marc is a good boy. Well look, Lee, I've told you the position I'm in. Now I'm counting on you to get me out of this spot. I've *got to* transmit my report to Council within a week. I don't want to pressure you, but you know I'm in a position to do it if I have to. Dammit, give me a report."

"I'll turn something in in a few days," Rynason said vaguely. His brain was definitely fuzzy now from the tarpaq.

Manning stood up. "All right, don't forget it. Trick it out with some high-sounding guesses if you have to, like I said. Right now I've got to see a man about a woman." He paused, glancing at Mara. "You're busy?"

"I'm busy, yes." Her face was studiedly expressionless.

He shrugged briefly and went out, pushing and weaving his way through the hubbub that filled the bar. It was dark outside; Rynason caught a glimpse of the dark street as Manning went through the door. Night fell quickly on Hirlaj, with the suddenness of age.

Rynason turned back to the table, and Mara. He looked at her curiously.

"What were you doing with him, anyway? You usually keep to yourself."

The girl smiled wryly. She had deep black hair which fell to her shoulders in soft waves. Most of the women here grew their hair down to their waists, in exaggerated imitation of inner-world styles, but Mara had more taste than that. Her eyes were a clear brown, and they met his directly. "He was in a sharp mood, so I came along as peacemaker. You don't seem to have needed me."

"You helped, at that; thanks. Was that true about the governorship?"

"Of course. Manning seldom brags, you should know that. He's a very capable man, in some ways."

Rynason frowned. "He could be a lot more useful on this survey if he'd use his talents on tightening up the survey itself. He's forcing a premature report, and it isn't going to be worth much."

"Is that what's really bothering you?" she asked.

He tried to focus on her through the haze of the noisy bar. "Of course it is. That, and his whole attitude toward these people."

"The Hirlaji? Are they people to you?"

He shrugged. "What are people? Humans? Or reasoning beings you can talk to, communicate with?"

"I should think people would be reasoning beings you could relate to," she said softly. "Not just intellectually, but emotionally too. You have to be able to understand them to communicate that way—that's what makes people."

Rynason was silent, trying to integrate that into the fog in his head. The raucous noise of the bar had faded into an underwater murmur around him, lost somewhere where he could not see.

Finally, he said, "That's the trouble with them, the Hirlaji. I can't really understand them. It's like there's really no contact, not even through the interpreter." He stared into his drink. "I wish to hell we had some straight telepathers here; they might work with the Hirlaji, since they're telepathic anyway. I'd like to make a direct link myself."

After a few fleeting moments he felt Mara's hand on his arm, and realized that he had almost fallen asleep on the table.

"You'd better go on back to your quarters," she said.

He sat up, shaking his head to clear it. "No, but really—what do you think of that idea? What if I had a telepather, and I could link minds with Horng? Straight linkage, no interpreter in the middle. I could get right at that race memory myself!"

"I think you need to get some sleep," she said. She seemed to be a little worried. "I think you're getting too wrapped up in this thing. And forget about the telepathers."

Rynason looked at her and grinned. "Why?" he said quietly. "There's no harm in wishing."

"Because," she said, "we've got three telepathers coming in the day after tomorrow."

CHAPTER THREE

Rynason continued to smile at her for several seconds, until her words penetrated. Then he abruptly sat up and steadied himself with one hand against the edge of the table.

"Can you get one for me?"

She gave a reluctant shrug. "If you insist, and if Manning okays it. But is it a good idea? Direct contact with a mind so alien?"

As a matter of fact, now that he was faced with the actual possibility of it, he wasn't so sure. But he said, "We'll only know once we've tried it."

Mara dropped her eyes and swirled her drink, watching the tiny red spots form inside the glass and rise to the surface. There was a brief silence between them.

"*Repent*, Lee Rynason!" The words burst upon his ears over the waves of sound that filled the room. He turned, half-rising, to find Rene Malhomme hovering over him, his wide grin showing a tooth missing in the bottom row.

Rynason settled back into his chair. "Don't shout. I'm going to have a headache soon enough."

Malhomme took the chair which Manning had vacated and sat in it heavily. He set his hand-lettered placard against the edge of the table and leaned forward, waving a thick finger.

"You consort with men who would enslave the pure in heart!" he rumbled, but Rynason didn't miss the laughter in his eye.

"Manning?" he nodded. "He'd enslave every pure heart on this planet, if he could find one. As a matter of fact, I think he's already working on Mara here."

Malhomme turned to her and sat back, appraising her boldly. Mara met his gaze calmly, raising her eyebrows slightly as she waited for his verdict.

Malhomme shook his head. "If she's pure, then it's a sin," he said. "A thrice-damned sin, Lee. Have I ever expostulated to you upon the Janus-coin that is good and evil?"

"Often," Rynason said.

Malhomme shrugged and turned again to the girl. "Nevertheless," he said, "I greet you with pleasure."

"Mara, this is Rene Malhomme," Rynason said wearily. "He imagines that we're friends, and I'm afraid he's right."

Malhomme dipped his shaggy head. "The name is from the Old French of Earth—badman. I have a long and dishonorable family history, but the earliest of my ancestors whom I've been able to trace had the same name. Apparently there were too many Smiths, Carpenters, Bakers and Priests on that world—the time was ripe for a Malhomme. My first name would have been pronounced Reh-*nay* before the language reform dropped all accent marks from Earth tongues."

"Considering your background," Mara smiled, "you're in good company out here."

"Good company!" Malhomme cried. "I'm not looking for good company! My work, my mission calls me to where men's hearts are the blackest, where repentance and redemption are needed—and so I come to the Edge."

"You're religious?" she asked.

"Who *is* religious in these days?" Malhomme asked, shrugging. "Religion is of the past; it is dead. It is nearly forgotten, and one hears God's name spoken now in anger. God damn you, cry the masses! *That* is our modern religion!"

"Rene wanders around shouting about sin," Rynason explained, "so that he can take up collections to buy himself more to drink."

Malhomme chuckled. "Ah, Lee, you're shortsighted. I'm an unbeliever, and a black rogue, but at least I have a mission. Our scientific advance has destroyed religion; we've penetrated to the heavens, and found no God. But science has not *dis*proved Him, either, and people forget that. I speak with the voice of the forgotten; I remind people of God, to even the scales." He stopped talking long enough to grab the arm of a passing waiter and order a drink. Then he turned back to them. "Nothing says I have to *believe* in religion. If that were necessary, no one would preach it."

"Have you been preaching to the Hirlaji?" Rynason asked.

"An admirable idea!" Malhomme said. "Do they have souls?"

"They have a god, at least. Or used to, anyway. Fellow named Kor, who was god, essence, knowledge, and several other things all rolled into one."

"Return to Kor!" Malhomme said. "Perhaps it will be my next mission."

"What's your mission now?" Mara asked, smiling in spite of herself. "Besides your apparently lifelong study and participation in sin, I mean."

Malhomme sighed and sat back as his drink arrived. He dug into the pouch strung from his waist and flipped a coin to the waiter. "Believe it or not, I have one," he said, and his voice was now low and serious. "I'm not just a lounger, a drifter."

"What are you?"

"I am a spy," he said, and raised his glass to drain half of it with one swallow.

Mara smiled again, but he didn't return it. He sat forward and turned to Rynason. "Manning has been busily wrapping up the appointment for the governorship here," he said. "You probably know that."

Rynason nodded. The headache he had been expecting was already starting.

"Did you also know that he's been buying men here to stand with him in case someone else is appointed?" He glanced at Mara. "I go among the men every day, talking, and I hear a lot. Manning will end up in control here, one way or another, unless he's stopped."

"Buying men is nothing new," Rynason said. "In any case, is there a better man on the planet?"

Malhomme shook his head. "I don't know; sometimes I give up on the human race. Manning at least has a little culture in him—but he's more vicious than he seems, nevertheless. If he gets control here…"

"It will be no worse than any of the other planets out here," Rynason concluded for him.

"Except for one thing, perhaps—the Hirlaji. I don't have much against men killing each other…that's their own business. But unless we get somebody better than Manning governing here, the Hirlaji will be wiped out. The men here are already talking … they're afraid of them."

"Why? The Hirlaji are harmless."

"Because of their size, and because we don't know anything about them. Because they're intelligent—any uneducated man is afraid of intelligence, and when it's an alien…" He shook his head. "Manning isn't helping the situation."

"What do you mean by that?" Mara asked.

Malhomme's frown deepened, creasing the dark lines of his forehead into furrows. "He's using the Hirlaji as bogey-men. Says he's the only man on the planet who knows how to deal with them safely. Oh, you should hear him when he moves among his people…. I envy his ability to control them with words. A little backslapping, a joke or two—most of them I was telling last year—and he talks to them man to man, very friendly." He shook his head again. "Manning is so friendly with this scum that his attitude is nothing short of patronizing."

Rynason smiled wearily at Malhomme; for all the man's wildness, he couldn't help liking him. It had been like this every time he had run into him, on a dozen of the Edge-worlds. Malhomme, dirty and cynical, moved among the dregs of the stars preaching religion and fighting the corporations, the opportunists, the phony rebels who wanted nothing for anyone but themselves. He had been known to break heads together with his huge fists, and he had no qualms about stealing or even killing when his anger was aroused. Yet there was a peculiar honesty about him.

"You always have to have a cause, don't you, Rene?"

The greying giant shrugged. "It makes life interesting, and it makes me feel good sometimes. But I don't overestimate myself: I'm scum, like the rest of them. The only difference is that I know it; I'm just one man, with no more rights than anyone else, except those I can take." He held up his large knuckled hands and turned them in front of his face. "I've got broken bones in both of them. I wonder if the Buddha or the Christ ever hit a man. The books on religion that are left in the repositories don't say."

"Would it make any difference if they hadn't?" Rynason asked.

"Hell, no! I'm just curious." Malhomme stood up, hefting his repentance sign in the crook of one big arm. His face again took on its arched look as he said, "My duty calls me elsewhere. But I leave you with a message from the scriptures, and it has been my guiding light. 'Resist not evil,' my children. Resist not evil."

"Who said that?" Rynason asked.

Malhomme shook his head. "Damned if I know," he muttered, and went away.

After a moment Rynason turned back to the girl; she was still watching Malhomme thread his way through the men on his way to the door.

"So now you've met my spiritual father," he said.

Her deep brown eyes flickered back to his. "I wish I could use a telepather on him. I'd like to know how he really thinks."

"He thinks exactly as he speaks," Rynason said. "At least, at the moment he says something, he believes in it."

She smiled. "I suppose that's the only possible explanation for him." She was silent for a moment, her face thoughtful. Then she said, "He didn't finish his drink."

"You're all hooked up," the girl said. "Nod or something when you're ready." She was bent over the telepather, double checking the connectives and the blinking meters. Rynason and Horng sat opposite each other, the huge dark mound of the alien looming silently over the Earthman.

He never seemed upset, Rynason thought, looking up at him. Except for that one time when they'd run into the stone wall of the block on Tebron, Horng had displayed a completely even temperament—unruffled, calm, almost disinterested. But of course if the aliens had been completely uninterested in the Earthmen's probings at their history they would never have cooperated so readily; the Hirlaji were not animals to be ordered about by the Earthmen. Probably the codification of their history would prove useful to the aliens too; they had never arranged the race memory into a very coherent order themselves.

Not that that was surprising, Rynason decided. The Hirlaji had no written language—their telepathic abilities had made that unnecessary—and organization of material into neatly outlined form was a characteristic as much of the Earth languages as of Terran mentality. Such organization was not a Hirlaji trait apparently, at least not now in the twilight of their civilization. The huge aliens lived dimly through these centuries, dreaming in their own way of the past … and their way was not the Earthmen's.

So if they cooperated with the survey team on codifying and recording their history, who was the servant?

Well, with the direct linkage of minds the work should go faster. Rynason looked up at Mara and nodded, and she flicked the connection on the telepather.

Suddenly, like being overwhelmed by a breaking wave of seawater, Rynason felt Horng's mind envelope him. A torrent of thoughts, memories, pictures and concepts poured over him in a jumble; the sensory sensations of the alien came to him sharply, and memories that were strange, ideas that were incomprehensible, all in a sudden rush upon his mind. He fought down the fear that had leapt in him, gritted his teeth and waited for the wave to subside.

It did not subside; it settled. As the two minds, Earthman and Hirlaji, met in direct linkage they became almost one. Gradually Rynason could begin to see some pattern to the impressions of the alien. The picture of himself came first: he was small and angular, sitting several feet below Horng's—or his own—eyes; but more than that, he was not merely light, but pallid, not merely small, but fragile. The alien's view of reality, even through his direct sensations, was not merely visual or tactile but interpreted automatically in his own terms.

The odor of the hall in which they sat was different, the very temperature warmer. Rynason could see himself reeling on the stone bench where he sat, and Mara, strangely distorted, put out a hand to steady him. At the same time he was seeing through his own eyes, feeling her hand on his shoulder. But the alien sensations were stronger; their very strangeness commanded the attention of his mind.

He righted himself, physically and mentally, and began to probe tentatively in this new part of his mind. He could feel Horng too reaching slowly for contact; his presence was comfortable, mild, confused but unworried. As his thoughts blended with Horng's the present faded perceptibly; this confusion was merely a moment in centuries, and soon too it would pass. Rynason could feel himself relaxing.

Now he could reach out and touch the strange areas of this mind: the concepts and attitudes of an alien race and culture and experience. Everything became dim and dream-like: the Earthmen possibly didn't exist, the dry wastes of Hirlaj had always been here or perhaps once they had been green but through four generations the Large Hall had stood thus and the animals changed by the day too fast to distinguish them even under Kor if he should be reached ... why? there was no reason. There was no purpose, no goal, no necessity, no wishing, questing, hoping ... no curiosity. All would pass. All was passing even now; perhaps already it was gone.

Rynason shifted where he sat, reaching for the feeling of the stone bench beneath him for equilibrium, pulling out of Horng's thoughts and going back in almost immediately.

A chaos of mind enveloped him, but he was beginning to familiarize himself with it now. He probed slowly for the memories, down through Horng's own personal memories of three centuries, dry feet on the dust and low winds, down to the racial pool. And he found it.

Even knowing the outlines of the race's history did not help Rynason to place and correlate those impressions which came to him one on top of another, overlapping, merging, blending. He saw buildings which towered over him, masses of his people moving quietly around him, and thoughts came to him from their minds. He was Norhib, artisan, working slowly day by ... he was Rashanah, approaching the Gate of the Wall and looking ... he was Lohreen discussing the site where...he was digging the ground, pushing the heavy cart, lying on the pelt of animals, demolishing the building which would soon fall, instructing a child in balance.

A dirt-caked street stretched before him by night, the stones individually cut and smooth with the passage of heavy feet. "Tomorrow we will set out for the Region of Chalk while there is still time." A mind-voice from a Hirlaji hundreds, perhaps thousands of years old, dead but alive in the race-memory. Rynason could feel the whole personality there, in the memories, but he passed on.

"Murba has said that the priests will take him."

"There is no need for planting this year ... the soil is dry. There is no purpose."

"The child's mind is ready for war."

He felt Horng himself watching him, beside him or behind him ... nearby, anyway. The alien heard and saw with him, and stayed with him like a protector. Rynason felt his presence warmly: the calm of the alien continued to relax him. Old leather mother-hen, he thought, and Horng beside him seemed almost amused.

Suddenly he was Tebron.

Tebron Marl, prince in the Region of Mines, young and strong and ambitious. Rynason caught and held those impressions; he felt the muscles ripple strangely through his body as Tebron stretched, felt the cold wind of the flat cut through his loose garment. It was night, and he stood on the parapet of a heavy stone structure looking down across the immense stretch of the Flat, spotted here and there by lights. He controlled all this land, and would control more...

He was Tebron again, marching across the Flat at the head of an army. Metal weapons hung at the sides of his men, crudely fashioned bludgeons and jagged-edged swords, all quickly forged in the workshops of the Region of Mines. The babble of mind voices swelled around him, fear and anger and boredom, dull resentment, and other emotions Rynason could not identify. They were marching on the City of the Temple...

He slipped sideways in Tebron's mind, and suddenly he was in the middle of the battle. There was dust all around, kicked up by the scuffling feet of the huge warriors, and his breath came in gasps. Mind-voices shouted and screamed but he paid no attention; he swung his bludgeon over his head with a ferocity that made it whistle with a low sound in the wind. One of the defenders broke through the line around him, and he brought the bludgeon smashing down at him before he could thrust with his sword; the warrior fell to one side at the last moment and took the blow along one arm. He could feel the pain in his own mind, but he ignored it. Before the warrior could bring up his sword again Tebron crushed his head with the bludgeon, and the scream of pain in his own head disappeared. He heard the grunting and gasps of his own warriors and the clash of bodies and weapons around him...

The Hirlaji could not really be moving so quickly, Rynason thought; it must be that to Tebron it seemed so. They were quiet, slow-moving creatures. Or had they degenerated physically through the centuries? Still smelling the sweat of battle, he found Tebron's mind again.

There was still fighting in the city, but it was far away now; he heard it with the back of his mind as he mounted the steps of the Temple. Those were mop-up operations, clearing the streets of the last of the priest-king forces; he was not needed there. He had, to all intents, controlled the city since the night before, and had slept in the palace itself. Now it was time for the Temple.

He mounted the heavy, steep steps slowly, three guards at his back and three in front of him. The priests would be gone from the Temple, but there might be one or two last-ditch defenders remaining, and they would be armed with the Weapons of Kor ... hand-weapons which shot dark beams that could disintegrate anything in their path. They would be dangerous. Well, there would be no temple-guards in the inner court; his own men could remain outside to take care of them while he went in.

He stopped halfway up the steps and lifted his head to gaze up at the Temple walls rising above him. They were solid stone, built in the fashion of the Old Ones... smooth-faced except for the carvings above the entrance itself. They too were in the traditional style, copied exactly from the older buildings which had been built thousands of years ago, before the Hirlaji had even developed telepathy. The symbols of Kor ... so now at last he saw them.

Tomorrow he would effect a mass-linkage of minds and broadcast his orders for reconstruction. That would mean staying up all night preparing the communication, for it was impossible to maintain complete planet-wide linkage for too long and Tebron had many plans. Perhaps it would be possible to find a way to extend the duration of mass-linkages if the science quest could be pushed forward fast enough.

But that was tomorrow's problem—today, right now, it was right that he enter the Temple. It was not only symbolic of his assumption of power, but necessary religiously: every new ruler leader within the memory of the race had received sanction from Kor first.

A momentary echo-whisper of another mind touched his, and he whirled to his right to see one of the temple-guards in the shadows; he had been unable to successfully shield his thoughts. Tebron dropped to the ground and sent a quick, cool order to his own guards: "Kill him." The heavy, dark warriors stepped forward as the guard tried to shrink back further into the shadows. He was trapped.

But not unarmed. As he dropped to the steps and rolled quickly to one side Tebron heard the low vibration of a disintegrator beam pass over his shoulder and the crack of the wall behind him as it struck. And then the guards were on the warrior in the shadows.

They had brought down several of the temple-guards the night before, and commandeered their weapons. In a matter of moments this one fell too, his head and most of his trunk gone. One of the warriors shoved the half-carcass down the stairs, and bent forward at the knees to pick up his fallen weapon.

So now they had all fourteen of them; if any more of the temple-guards remained they could be dealt with easily. Tebron rose from the steps and wished momentarily that those weapons could be duplicated; if his whole army could be equipped with them... But after today that would probably be unnecessary; the entire planet was his now.

He walked up the last few steps and stepped into the shadows of the Temple of Kor...

The walls melted around him and Rynason felt his mind wrenched painfully. There was a screaming all through him, thin and high, blotting out the contact he had held with Tebron's mind. It was Horng's scream, beside him, overpowering. Terror washed over him; he tried to fight it but he couldn't. The shadows of the walls twisted and faded, Tebron's thoughts disappeared, and all that remained was the screaming and the fear, like a mouth open wide against his ear and hot breath shouting into him. He felt his stomach turn and nausea and vertigo threw him panting out of Tebron's mind.

Yet Horng was still beside him in the darkness, and as the echoes faded he felt him there ... alien, but calm. There had been fear in this huge alien mind, but it had disappeared almost immediately with the breaking of the connection with Tebron. All that remained in Horng's mind now was a dull quietness.

Rynason felt a rueful grin on his face, and he said, perhaps aloud and perhaps not, "You haven't forgotten what happened here, old leather. The memories are there, all right."

From Horng's mind came a slow rebuilding of the fear that he had just experienced, but it subsided. And as it did Rynason probed again into his mind, searching quickly for that contact he had just lost. He could almost feel Tebron's mind, began to see the darkness forming the wall-shadows, when again there was a blast of the terror and he felt his mind reeling back from those memories. The screaming filled his mind and body and this time he felt Horng himself blocking him, pushing him back.

But there was no need for that; the fear was not Horng's alone. Rynason felt it too, and he retreated before its onslaught with an overpowering need to preserve his own sanity.

When the darkness subsided Rynason became aware of himself still sitting on the stone bench, sweat drenching his body. Horng sat before him in the same position he had been in when they had started; it was as if nothing had happened at all. Rynason wearily raised one hand and motioned to Mara to break the linkage.

She switched off the telepather and gingerly removed the wires from his head, frowning worriedly at him. But she waited for him to speak.

He grinned at her after a moment and said, "It was a bit rough in there. We couldn't break through."

She was removing the wires from Horng, who sat unmoving, staring dully over Rynason's shoulder at the wall behind him. "You should have seen yourself when you were under," she said. "I wanted to break the connection before, but I wasn't sure…"

Rynason sat forward and flexed the muscles of his shoulders and back. They ached as though they had been tense for an hour, and his stomach was still knotted tight.

"There's a real block there," he said. "It's like a thousand screaming birds flapping in your face. When you get that far into his mind, you feel it too." He sat staring down at his feet, exhausted mentally and physically.

She sat on the bench and looked closely at him. "Anything else?"

"Yes—Horng. At the end, the second time I went in, I could feel him, not only fighting me, but … hating me." He looked up at her. "Can you imagine actually feeling him, right next to you in your mind like you were one person, hating you?"

Across from them, the huge figure of the alien slowly stood up and looked at them for several long seconds, then turned and left the building.

CHAPTER FOUR

Manning's quarters were larger than most of the prefab structures in the new Earth town; the building was out near the end of one of the streets, a single-storied plastic-and-metal box on a quick-concrete slab base. Well, it was as well constructed as any of the buildings in the Edge planetfalls, Rynason reflected as he knocked on the door. And there was room for all of the survey team workers.

Manning himself let him in, grabbing his hand in a firm grip that nevertheless lacked the man's usual heavy joviality. "Come on in; the others are already here," Manning said, and walked ahead of him into the larger of the two rooms inside. His step was brisk as always, but there was a touch of real hurry in it which Rynason noticed immediately. Manning was worried about something.

"All right; we're all set," Manning said, leaning against a wall at the front of the room. Rynason found a seat on the arm of a chair next to Mara and Marc Stoworth, a slightly heavy, blond-haired man in his thirties who wore his hair cut short on the sides but long in back. He looked like every one of the young corporation executives Rynason had seen in the outworlds, and probably would have gone into that kind of position if he'd had the connections. He certainly seemed out of place even among the varied assortment of types who worked the archaeological and geological surveys ... but these surveys were conducted by the big corporations who were interested in developing the outworlds; probably Stoworth hoped eventually to move up into the lower management offices when the corporations moved in.

"Gentlemen, there's something very wrong about these dumb horses we've been dealing with," Manning said. "I'm going to throw out a few facts at you and see if you don't come to the same conclusions that Larsborg and I did."

Rynason leaned over to Mara and murmured, "What's his problem today?"

But she was frowning. "He's got a real one. Listen."

Manning had picked up a sheaf of typescript from the table next to him and was flipping through it, his lips pursed grimly. "This is the report I got yesterday from Larsborg here—architecture and various other artifacts. It's very interesting. Herb, throw that first photo onto the screen."

The lights went off and the screen in the wall beside Manning lit up with a reproduction of one of the Hirlaji structures out on the Flat. It stood in the shadow of an overhanging rock-cliff, protected from the planet's heavy winds on three sides. Larsborg had apparently set up lights for a clearer picture; the whole building stood out sharply against the shadows of the background.

"This look familiar to any of you?" Manning said quietly.

For just a moment Rynason continued to stare uncomprehending at the picture. He had seen a lot of the Hirlaji buildings since they'd landed; this one was better preserved but not essentially different in design. Larsborg had cleared away most of the dirt and sand which had been packed up against its sides, exposing the full height of the structure, and he'd apparently sand-blasted the carved designs over the entrance, but...

Then he realized what he was seeing. The angle of the photo was a bit different than that from which he'd seen the other structure back on Tentar XI, but the similarity was unmistakable. This was a reproduction in stone of that same building, the one they'd reconstructed two years before.

He heard a wave of voices growing around the room, and Manning's voice cut-through it with: "That's right, gentlemen: it's an Outsiders building. It's not in that crazy, damned metal or alloy or whatever it was that they used, but it's the same design. Take a good long look at it before we go on to the next photo."

Rynason looked...closely. Yes, it was the same design a bit cruder, and the carvings weren't the same, but the lines of the doorway and the cornice...

The next picture flashed onto the screen. It was a closeup of the designs over the entrance, shot in sharp relief so that they stood out starkly. The room was so quiet that Rynason could hear the hum behind the screen in the wall.

"That's Outsiders stuff too," said Breune. "It's not quite the same, though ... distorted."

"It's carved in stone, not stamped in metal," Manning said. "It's the same thing, all right. Anybody disagree?"

No one did.

"All right, then; let's have the lights back up again."

The lights came on and once more there was a murmur of talking around the room. Rynason shifted his position on the seat and tried to catch the thought that had slipped through his mind just before the screen had faded. There was another similarity... Well, he'd seen a lot of the Outsider buildings in the past few years; it wasn't necessary to trace all the evidences right now.

"What I want to know is, why didn't any of the rest of you see this?" said Manning angrily. "Have you all got plastic for brains? Over a dozen men spend weeks researching these damn horsefaces, and only one of you has the sense to see the evidence of his own eyes!"

"Maybe we should turn in our spades," said Stoworth.

Manning glared at him. "Maybe you should, if you think this isn't serious. Let's get this clear: these old horsefaces that so many of you think are just as quaint as can be have been building in exactly the same style as the Outsiders. Quaint, are they? Harmless too, I suppose!"

He stood with his hands on his hips, dropped his head and took a long, deep breath. When he looked up again his forehead was furrowed into an intense frown. "Gentlemen … as I call you from force of habit … we've been finding dead cities of the Outsiders for centuries. They were all over God knows how many galaxies before your ancestors or mine had stopped playing with their tails; as far as we can tell they had a civilization as tightly-knit as our own, and probably stronger. And sometime about forty thousand years ago they started pulling out. They left absolutely nothing behind but empty buildings and a few crumbling bits of machinery. And we've been following those remains ever since we got out of our own star-system.

"Well, we just may have found them at last. Right here, on Hirlaj. Now what do you think of that?"

No one said anything for a minute. Rynason looked down at Mara, caught her smile, and stood up.

"I don't think the Hirlaji are the Outsiders," he said calmly.

Manning shot a sharp glance at him. "You saw the photos."

"Yes, I saw them. That's Outsiders work, all right, or something a lot like it. But it doesn't necessarily prove that thes...how many of them are there? Twenty-five? I don't think these creatures are the Outsiders. We've traced their history back practically to the point of complete barbarism. Their culture was never once high enough to get them off this planet, let alone to let them spread all over among the stars."

Manning waited for him to finish, then he turned back to the rest of the men in the room and spread his hands. "Now that, gentlemen, just shows how much we've found out so far." He looked over at Rynason again. "Has it occurred to you, Lee, that if these horses *are* the Outsiders, that maybe they know a little more than we do? I suppose you're going to say you had a telepathic hookup with one of them and you didn't see a thing to make you suspicious ... but just remember that they've been using telepathy for several thousand years and that you hardly know what you're doing when you try it.

"Look, I don't trust them—if they're the Outsiders they've got maybe a hundred thousand years head-start on us scientifically. There may be only a couple dozen of them, but we don't know how strong they are."

"That's if they're really the Outsiders," said Rynason.

Manning nodded his head impatiently. "Yes, that's what I'm saying. If they're the Outsiders, which looks like a sensible conclusion. Or do you have a better one?"

"Well, I don't know if it's better," said Rynason. "It may not even be as attractive, for that matter. But have you considered that maybe when the Outsiders pulled out of our area they simply moved on elsewhere? We're so used to seeing dead cities that we think automatically that the Outsiders must be dead too, which I suppose is what's bothering you about finding the Hirlaji here alive. But it might be worse. That whole empire could simply have moved on to this area; we could be on the edge of it right now, ready to run head-on into a hundred star systems just crowded with the Outsiders."

Manning stared at him, and the expression on his face was not quite anger. Something like it, but not anger.

"The ruins we've found here were built by the Hirlaji," Rynason said. "I saw them building when I was linked with Horng, and these are the same structures. But the design was copied from older buildings, and I don't know how far back I'd have to search the memories before I found where they originally got that kind of approach to design. Maybe back before they developed telepathy. But this race simply isn't as old as the Outsiders; they came out of barbarism thousands of years after the Outsiders had left those dead cities we've been finding. The chances are that if the Hirlaji were influenced by the Outsiders it was sometime around thirty thousand years ago … which means the Outsiders came this way when they left those cities. That would mean that we're following them … and we might catch up at any time."

He stopped for a moment, then said, "We're moving faster than they were, and we have no idea where they may have settled again. One more starfall further beyond the Edge, and we may run into one of their present outposts. But this isn't it. Not yet."

Manning was still staring at Rynason, but it was a curious stare. "You're pretty sure that what you've been getting out of that horseface's head is real?" he asked levelly. "You trust them?"

Rynason nodded. "Horng was really afraid; that was real. I felt it myself. And the rest of it was real, too—I could see the whole racial memory there, and nobody could have been making that up. If you'd experienced that…"

"Well, I didn't," Manning said shortly. "And I don't think I trust them." He paused, and after a moment frowned. "But this direct linkage business does seem to be the best way we have of checking on them. I want you to get busy, Lee, and go after that horse's thoughts for us. Don't let him drive you out again; if he's hiding something, get in there and see what it is. Above all, don't trust him.

"If these things are the Outsiders, they could be bluffing us."

Manning stopped talking, and thought a minute. He looked up under raised eyebrows at Rynason. "And be careful, Lee. I'm counting on you."

Rynason ignored his paternal gaze, and turned instead to Mara. "We'll try it again tomorrow," he said. "Get in a requisition for a telepather this afternoon; make sure we'll have one ready to go first thing in the morning. I'll check back with you about an hour after we leave here today."

She looked up at him, surprised. "Check back? Why?"

"I put in a requisition myself, yesterday. Wine from Cluster II, vintage '86. I was hoping for some company."

She smiled. "All right."

Manning was ending the session. "…Carl, be sure to get those studies of the Outsiders artifacts together for me by tonight. And I'm going to hand back your reports to each of the rest of you; go through them and watch for those inconsistencies you skipped over the first time. We may be able to turn up something else that doesn't check out. Go over them *carefully*—all the reports were sloppy jobs. You're all trying to work too fast."

Rynason rose with the rest of them, grinning as he remembered how Manning had rushed those reports. Well, that was one of the privileges of authority: delegating fault. He started for the door.

"Lee! Hold it a minute; I want to talk to you, alone."

Rynason sat, and when all the others had gone Manning came back and sat down opposite him. He slowly took out a cigaret and lit it.

"My last pack till the next spacer makes touchdown," he said. "Sorry I can't offer you one, but I'm a fiend for the things. I know they're supposed to be non-habit-forming these days, but I'm a man of many vices."

Rynason shrugged, waiting for him to come to the point.

"I guess it makes me a bit more open-minded about what the members of my staff do," Manning went on. "You know—why should I crack down on drinking or smoking, for instance, when I do it myself?"

"I'm glad you see it that way," Rynason said drily. "Why did you want me to stay?"

Manning exhaled a long plume of smoke slowly, watching it through narrowed eyes. "Well, even though I'm pretty easy going about things, I do try to keep an eye on you. When you come right down to it, I'm responsible for every man who's with me out here." He stopped, and laughed shortly. "Not that I'm as altruistic as that sounds, of course—you know me, Lee. But when you're in a position of authority you have to face the responsibilities. You understand me?"

"You have to protect your own reputation back at Cluster headquarters," Rynason said.

"Well, yes. Of course, you get into a pattern of thinking eventually…sort of a fatherly feeling, I suppose, though

I've never even been on the parentage rolls back on the in-worlds. But I mean it—it happens, I get that feeling. And I'm getting a bit worried about you, Lee."

Rynason could see what was coming now. He sat further back into the chair and said, "Why?"

Manning frowned with concern. "I've been noticing you with Mara lately. You seem pretty interested in her."

"Is she one of those vices you were telling me about, Manning?" said Rynason quietly. "You want to warn me to stay away from her?"

Manning shook his head, a quick gesture dismissing the idea. "No, Lee, not at all. She's not that kind of a woman. And that's my point. I can see how you look at her, and you're on the wrong track. When you're out here on the Edge, you don't want a wife."

"What I need is some good healthy vice, is that what you mean?"

Manning sat forward. "That puts it pretty clearly. Yeah, that's about it. Lee, you're building up some strong tensions on this job, and don't think I'm not aware of it. Telepathing with that horseface is getting rough, judging from what you've told me. I think you should go get good and drunk and kick up hell tonight. And take one of the town women; they're always available. Do you good, I mean it."

Rynason stood up. "Maybe tomorrow night," he said. "Tonight I'm busy. With Mara." He turned and walked toward the door.

"I'd suggest you get busy with someone else," Manning said quietly behind him. "I'm really telling you this for your own good, believe it or not."

Rynason turned at the door and regarded the man coldly. "She's not interested in you, Manning," he said. He went out and shut the door calmly behind him.

Manning could be irritating with his conceited posing, but his veiled threats didn't bother Rynason. In any case, he had something else on his mind just now. He had finally remembered what it had been about the carvings over the Hirlaji building in the photo that had touched a memory within him: there was a strong similarity to the carvings that he had seen, through Tebron's eyes, outside the Temple of Kor. The symbols of Kor, Tebron had called them ... copied from the works of the Old Ones.

The Outsiders?

CHAPTER FIVE

They had some trouble getting cooperation from Horng on any further mind-probing. The Hirlaji lived among some of the ruins out on the Flat, where the winds threw dust and sand against the weathered stone walls, leaving them worn smooth and rounded. The aliens kept these buildings in some state of repair, and there was a communal garden of the planet's dark, fungoid plant life. As Rynason and Mara strode between the massive buildings they passed several of the huge creatures; one or two of them turned and regarded the couple with dull eyes, and went on slowly through the grey shadows.

They found Horng sitting motionlessly at the edge of the cluster of buildings, gazing out over the Flat toward the low hills which stood black against the deep blue of the horizon sky. Rynason lowered the telepather from his shoulder and approached him.

The alien made no motion of protest when Rynason hooked up the interpreter, but when the Earthman raised the mike to speak, Horng's dry voice spoke in the silence of the thin air and the machine's stylus traced out, THERE IS NO PURPOSE.

Rynason paused a moment, then said, "We're almost finished with our reports. We should finish today."

THERE IS NO PURPOSE MEANING QUEST.

"No purpose to the report?" Rynason said after a moment. "It's important to us, and we're almost finished. There would be even less purpose in stopping now, when so much has been done."

Horng's large, leathery head turned toward him and Rynason felt the ancient creature's heavy gaze on him like a shadow.

WE ARE ACCUSTOMED TO THAT.

"We don't think alike," Rynason said to him. "To me there is a purpose. Will you help me once more?"

There was no answer from the alien, only a slow nodding of his head to one side, which Rynason took for assent. He motioned Mara to set up the telepather.

After their last experience Rynason could understand the creature's reluctance to continue. Perhaps even his statement that there was no purpose to the Earthmen's researches made sense—for could the codification of the history of a dying race mean much to its last members? Probably they didn't care; they walked slowly through the ruins of their world and felt all around them fading, and the jumbled past in their minds must be only one more thing that was to disappear.

And Rynason had not forgotten the terrified waves of hatred which had blasted at him in Horng's mind—nor had Horng, he was sure.

Mara connected the leads of the telepather while the alien sat motionlessly, his dark eyes only occasionally watching either of them. When she was finished Rynason nodded for her to activate the linkage.

Then there was the rush of Horng's mind upon his, the dim thought-streams growing closer, the greyed images becoming sharper and washing over him, and in a moment he felt his own thoughts merge with them, felt the totality of his own consciousness blend with that of Horng. They were together; they were almost one mind.

And in Horng he heard the whisper of distrust, of fear, and the echoes of that hatred which had struck at him once before. But they were in the background; all around him here on the surface was a pervading feeling of… uselessness, resignation, almost of unreality. The calm which he had noted before in Horng had been shaken and turned, and in its place was this fog of hopelessness.

Tentatively, Rynason reached for the racial memories in that grey mind, feeling Horng's own consciousness heavy beside him. He found them, layers of thoughts of unknown aliens still alive here, the pictures and sounds of thousands of years past. He probed among them, looking again for the memories of Tebron…and found what he was searching for.

He was Tebron, marching across that vast Flat which he had seen before, the winds alive around him among the shuffling feet of his army. He felt the muscles of his massive legs tight with weariness, and tasted the dryness of the air as he drew in long gasps. He was still hours from the City, but they would rest before dawn….

Rynason turned among those memories, moving forward in them, and was aware of Horng watching him. There was still the wariness in his mind, and a stir of anxiety, but it was blanketed by the tired hopelessness he had seen. He reached further in the memories, and…

The temple-guard fell in the shadows, and one of his own warriors stepped forward to retrieve his weapon. The remains of the guard's body rolled down three, four, five of the steps of the Temple, and stopped. His eyes lingered on that body for only a moment, and then he turned and went up to the entrance.

There was a moaning of pain, or of fright, rising somewhere in his head; he was only partly aware of it. He walked into the shadows of the doorway and paused. But only for a moment: there was no movement inside, and he stepped forward, down one step into the interior.

Screams echoed through the halls and corridors of the Temple—high and piercing, growing in volume as they echoed, buffeting him almost into unconsciousness. He knew they were from Horng, but he fought them, watching his own steps across the dark inner room. He was Tebron Marl, king priest ruler of all Hirlaj, in the Temple of Kor, and he could feel the stone solid beneath his feet. Sweat broke out on his back—his own, or Tebron's? But he *was* Tebron, and he fought the blast of fear in his mind as though it were a battle for his very identity. He *was* Tebron.

The screaming faded, and he stood in silence before the Altar of Kor.

So this is the source, he thought. For how many days had he fought toward this? It was useless to remember; the muscles of his body were remembrance enough, and the scar-tissue that hindered the movement of one shoulder. If he remembered those battles he would again hear the fading echoes of enemy minds dying within his, and he had had enough of that. This was the goal, and it was his; perhaps there need be no more such killing.

He opened his mouth and spoke the words which he had learned so many years before, during his apprenticeship in the Region of Mines. The rituals of the Temple were always conducted in the ancient spoken language; Kor demanded it, and only the priest-caste knew these words, for they were so old that their form had changed almost completely even by the time his people had developed telepathy and discarded speech; they were not communicated to the rest of the people.

"I am Tebron Marl, king priest leader of all Hirlaj. I await your orders guidance."

He knelt, according to ritual, and gazed up at the altar. The Eye of Kor blinked there, a small circle of light in the dark room. The altar was simple but massive; its heavy columns, built upon the traditional lines, supported the weight of the Eye. He watched its slow waxing and waning, and waited; within him, Rynason's mind stirred.

And Kor spoke.

Remain motionless. Do not go forward.

He felt a child as a wave of sensitivity spread through all of his skin and his organs sped for a moment. Then it was true: in the Temple of Kor, the god leader really did speak.

"I await further words."

The Eye held his gaze almost hypnotically in the dimness. The voice sounded in the huge arched room. *The sciences quests of your race lead you to extinction. The knowledge words offered to me by your priests make it clear that within a hundred years your race will leave its planet. You must not go forward, for that way lies the extermination of all your race.*

His mind swam; this was not what he had expected. The god leader Kor had always aided his people in their sciences; in the knowledge word offerings they reported to the Eye the results of their studies, and often, if asked properly, the god leader would clarify uncertainties which they faced. But now he ordered an ending to research quests. This was unthinkable! Knowledge was godhood; godhood was knowledge, of the essence; the essence was knowing understanding. To him, to his people, it was a unity—and now that unity repudiated itself. Faintly in the darkness somewhere he again heard screaming.

"Are we to abandon all progress? Are the stars so dangerous?"

The concept wish of progress must die within your people. There must be no purpose in any field of knowledge. You must remain motionless, consolidate what you have, and live in peace. The Eye in the dimness seemed larger and brighter the longer he looked at it; all else in the echoing room was darkness. *The stars are not dangerous, but there is a race which rises with you, and it rises more rapidly. Should you expand into the stars you will only meet that race sooner, and they will be stronger. They are more warlike than your people; already you are capable of peace, and that must be your aim. Remain on your world; consolidate; cultivate the fruits of your civilization as it is, but do not go forward. In that way, you will have five thousand years before that race finds you, and if you are no threat to them they will not destroy you.*

He felt a rising anger in him as the god leader's words came to him in the dark room, and a fear that lay deeper. He was a warrior, and a quester ... how could he give up all such pursuits, and how could he be expected to force all his people to do the same? There would be no hope wish of advance, no curiosity...no purpose.

"Is this other race so much more advanced than we are?" he asked.

He heard a low humming from the altar and the Eye grew brighter again. *They are not so much ahead of you now ... but they are more warlike, and will therefore develop more quickly. In both your races, war is a quest which you use as a release for what is in you. Your sciences questings and your wars are the same thing ... you must suppress both. They are discontentment, and you will find that only in peace, if at all.*

He dipped his head to one side, a gesture of acquiescence or agreement. He couldn't argue with the god leader Kor, and he had been wrong even to think of it.

"How am I to suppress the race? Is it possible to convince each of them of the necessity for abandoning forgetting all questing?"

The Eye hummed, and grew brighter against the darkness of the carved wall behind it, but it was some time before Kor spoke again. *It would be impossible to convince every one. The reasons must be kept from them, and kept from the shared memories; you must not communicate my knowledge words in any way. Consolidate your power, force peace upon them and lead them into acceptance. The knowledge questing can be made to die within them. Remember that there will be no purpose ... in that they must find contentment.*

The king priest leader of all Hirlaj waited a moment, and was ready to rise and leave when the Eye spoke again.

You must abolish the priesthood. The knowledge which I have given to you must die when you die.

He waited for a long time in the dim, suddenly cold hall for the god leader to speak again, then slowly rose and walked to the door, the image of the Eye of Kor still bright in his vision. He stopped outside the doorway, hearing the soft wind of the city flowing slowly past the stone archway above him. One of his guards reached out and touched his mind tentatively, but he blocked his thoughts and strode heavily down the steps past them.

The sound of the wind above him rose to a screaming, and suddenly it was as though he were tumbling down the entire length of the stairway, fragments of sky and stone and faces flashing past in a kaleidoscope, and the screaming all around him. He almost reached for his bludgeon, but then he realized that he was not Tebron Marl ... he was Lee Rynason, and the screaming was Horng and he was being driven out of those thoughts, tumbling through a thousand memories so fast he could not grasp any one of them.

He withdrew from Horng's mind as though from a nightmare; he became aware of his own body, lying in the dust of Hirlaj, and he opened his eyes and motioned weakly to Mara to break the connection.

When she had done so he slowly sat up and shook his head, waiting for it to clear. For awhile he had been an ancient king of Hirlaj, and it took some time to return to the present, to his own consciousness. He was dimly aware of Mara kneeling beside him, but he couldn't make out her words at first.

"Are you all right? Are you sure? Look up at me, Lee, please."

He found himself nodding to reassure her, and then he saw the expression on her face and felt the last wisps of alien fog clearing from his mind. There were tears in her eyes, and he touched the side of her face with his hand and said, "I'm all right. But why don't you kiss me or something?"

She did, but before Rynason could really immerse himself in it she broke away and said, "You must have had a bad time with him! It was as though you were dead."

He grinned a trifle sheepishly and said, "Well, it was engrossing. You'd better unhook the beast; he had a bad time of it too."

Mara rose and removed the wires from Horng gingerly. Rynason remained sitting; some of the meaning of what he had just experienced was coming to him now. It certainly explained why the Hirlaji had suddenly passed from their war era into lasting peace, and why the memories had been blocked. But could he credit those memories of a voice of an alien god?

And sitting in the dust at the edge of the vast Hirlaj plain the full realization came to him, as it could not when he had been Tebron. Not only the Temple, but the Altar of Kor itself had been unmistakably the workmanship of the Outsiders.

CHAPTER SIX

They left Horng sitting dully at the edge of the Flat and retraced their steps through the Hirlaji ruins, still drawing no notice from the aliens. Rynason had been in some of the small planetfall towns where settlements had been established only to be abandoned by the main flow of interstellar traffic...those backwater areas where contact with the parent civilization was so slight that an entirely local culture had developed, almost as different from that of the mainstream Terran colonies as was this last vestige of the Hirlaji civilization. And in some of those areas interest in Earth was so slight that the offworlders were ignored, as the Earthmen were here...but he had never felt the total lack of attention that was here. It was not as though the Hirlaji had seen the Earthmen and grown used to them; Rynason had the feeling that to the Hirlaji the Earthmen were no more important than the winds or the dust beneath their feet.

As they passed through the settled portion of the ruins Rynason had to step around a Hirlaji who crossed his path. He walked silently past, his eyes not even flickering toward the Earthlings. Crazy grey hidepiles, Rynason thought, and he and Mara hurried out across the Flat toward the nearby Earth town.

On the outskirts of the town, where the packed-dirt streets faded into loose dust and garbage was already piled several feet high, they were met by Rene Malhomme. He sat long-legged with his back leaning against a weathered stone outcropping. He seemed old already, though he was not yet fifty; his windblown hair was almost the color of the surrounding grey dust and rock—perhaps because it was filled with that dust, Rynason thought. He stopped and looked down at the worn, tired man whose eyes belied that weariness.

"And have you communicated with God, Lee Rynason?" Malhomme asked with his rumbling, sardonic voice.

Rynason met his gaze, wondering what he wanted. He lowered the telepather pack from his shoulder and set it in the dust. Mara sat on a low rock beside him.

"Will an alien god do?" Rynason said.

Malhomme's eyes rested on the telepather for a moment. "You spoke with Kor?" he asked.

Rynason nodded slowly. "I made a linkage with one of the Hirlaji, and tapped the race-memory. I suppose you could say I spoke with Kor."

"You have touched the alien godhead," Malhomme mused. "Then it's real? Their god is real?"

"No," said Rynason. "Kor is a machine."

Malhomme's head jerked up. "A machine? *Deus ex machina*, to quote an ancient curse. We make our own machines, and make gods of them." The tired lines of his face relaxed. "Well, that's a bit better. The gods remain a myth, and it's better that way."

Rynason stood over him on the windy Flat, still puzzled by his manner. He glanced at Mara, but she too was watching Malhomme, waiting for him to speak again.

Suddenly, Malhomme laughed, a dry laugh which almost rasped in his throat. "Lee Rynason, I have called men to God for so long that I almost began to believe it myself. And when the men started talking about the god of these aliens...." He shook his head, the spent laughter still drawing his mouth back into a grin. "Well, I'm glad it isn't true. Religion wouldn't be worth a damn if it were true."

"How did the men find out about Kor?" Rynason asked.

Malhomme spread his hands. "Manning has been talking, as usual. He ridicules the Hirlaji, and their god. And at the same time he says they are a menace."

"Why? Is he still trying to work the townsmen up against them?"

"Of course. Manning wants all the power he can get. If it means sacrificing the Hirlaji, he'll do it." Malhomme stood up, stretching himself. "He says they may be the Outsiders, and he's stirring up all the fear he can. He'll grab any excuse, no matter how impossible."

"It's not so impossible," Rynason said. "Kor is an Outsiders machine."

Malhomme stared at him. "You're sure of that?"

He nodded. "There's no doubt of it—I saw it from three feet away." He told Malhomme of his linkage with Horng, the contact with the memories, the mind, Tebron, and of the interview with the machine that was Kor. Malhomme listened with fascination, his shaggy head tilted to one side, occasionally throwing in a comment or a question.

As he finished, Rynason said, "That race that Kor warned them about sounds remarkably like us. A warlike race that would crush them if they left the planet. We haven't found any other intelligent life ... just the Hirlaji, and us."

"And the Outsiders," said Malhomme.

"No. This was a race which was still growing from barbarism, at about the same level as the Hirlaji themselves. Remember, the Outsiders had already spread through a thousand star-systems long before this. No, we're the race they were warned against."

"What about the weapons?" Malhomme said. "Disintegrators. We haven't got anything that powerful that a man can carry in his hand. And yet the Hirlaji had them thousands of years ago."

"Yes, but for some reason they couldn't duplicate them. It doesn't make sense: those weapons were apparently beyond the technological level of the Hirlaji, but they had them."

"Perhaps your aliens *were* the Outsiders," Malhomme said. "Perhaps we see around us the remnants of a great race fallen."

Rynason shook his head.

"But they must have had some contact with the Outsiders," Mara said. "Sometime even before Tebron's lifetime. The Outsiders could have left the disintegrators, and the machine that they thought was a god...."

"That's just speculation," Rynason said. "Tebron himself didn't really know where they'd come from; they'd been passed down through the priesthood for a long time, and within the priesthood they did have some secrets. I suppose if I could search the race-memory long enough I might find another nice big block there hiding that secret. But it's difficult."

"And you may not have time," Malhomme said. "When Manning hears that the Altar of Kor was an Outsiders machine, there'll be no way left to stop him from slaughtering the Hirlaji."

"I'm not sure there'll be any real trouble," Rynason said.

Malhomme's lips drew back into the deep lines of his face. "There is always trouble. Always. Whoever or whatever spoke through the machine knew that much about us. The only way you could stop it, Lee, would be to hold back this information from Manning. And to do that, you would have to be sure, yourself, that there is no danger from the Hirlaji. You're in the key position, right now."

Rynason frowned. He knew Malhomme was right—it would be difficult to stop Manning if what he'd said about the man's push for power was true. But could he be sure that the Hirlaji were as harmless as they seemed? He remembered the reassuring touch of Horng's mind upon his own, the calmness he found in it, and the resignation … but he also remembered the fear, and the screaming, and the hot rush of anger that had touched him.

In the silence on the edge of the Flat, Mara spoke. "Lee, I think you should report it all to Manning."

"Why?"

Her face was clouded. "I'm not sure. But … when I disconnected the wires of the telepather, Horng looked at me…. Have you ever looked into his eyes, up close? It's frightening: it makes you remember how old they are, and how strong. Lee, that creature has muscles in his face as strong as most men's arms!"

"He just looked at you?" said Rynason. "Nothing else?"

"That's all. But those eyes … they were so deep, and so full. You don't usually notice them, because they're set so deeply in the shadows of his face, but his eyes are *large*." She stopped, and shook her head in confusion. "I can't really explain it. When I moved around him to the other side, I could see his eyes following me. He didn't move, otherwise—it was as though only his eyes were alive. But they frightened me. There was much more in them than just … not seeing, or not caring. His eyes were alive."

"That's not much evidence to make you think the Hirlaji are dangerous."

"Oh, I don't *know* if they could be dangerous. But they're not just…passive. They're not vegetables. Not with those eyes."

"All right," Rynason said. "I'll give Manning a full report, and we'll put it in his hands."

He picked up the telepather pack and slung it over his shoulder. Mara stood up, shaking away the dust which had blown against her feet.

"What will you do," Malhomme asked, "if Manning decides that's enough cause to kill the Hirlaji?"

"I'll stop him," Rynason said. "He's not in control here, yet."

Malhomme flashed his sardonic smile again. "Perhaps not … but if you need help, call to God. The books say nothing about alien races, but surely these must be God's creatures too. And I'm always ready to break a few heads, if it will help." He turned and spat into the dust. "Or even just for the hell of it," he said.

Rynason found Manning that same afternoon, going over reports in his quarters. As soon as he began his description of the orders given to Tebron he found that Malhomme's warnings had been correct.

"What did this machine say about us?" Manning asked sharply. "Why were the Hirlaji supposed to stay away from us?"

"Because we're a warlike race. The idea was that if the Hirlaji stayed out of space they'd have about five thousand years before we found them."

"How long ago was all this? I had your report here…"

"At least eight thousand years," Rynason said. "They overestimated us."

Manning stood up, scowling. There were heavy lines around his eyes and he hadn't trimmed his thin beard.

Whatever he was working on, Rynason thought, he was putting a lot of effort into it.

"This doesn't make sense, Lee. Damn it, since when do machines make guesses? Wrong ones, at that?"

Rynason shrugged. "Well, you've got to remember that this was an alien machine; maybe that's the way they built them."

Manning threw a cold glance at him and poured a glass of Sector Three brandy for himself. "You're not being amusing," he said shortly. "Now, go on, and make some sense."

"I'd like to," Rynason said. "Frankly, my theory is that the machine was a communication-link with the Outsiders. It could explain a lot of things—maybe even the similarities in architecture."

Manning scowled and turned away from him. He paced heavily across the room and looked out through the plasticene window at the nearly empty, dust-strewn street for a few moments; when he returned the frown was still on his face.

"Damn it, Lee, you're not keeping your mind on the problems here. While you were looking into Horng's mind, how do you know he wasn't spying in yours? You had an equal hookup, right?"

Rynason nodded. "I couldn't have prevented him in any case. Why? Are we supposed to be hiding anything?"

"I told you not to trust them!" Manning snapped. "Now if you can't even match wits with a senile horsehead…"

"You were the one who said they might be more adept at telepathy than we are," Rynason said. "It was a chance we had to take."

"There's a difference between taking chances and handing them information on a silver platter," Manning said angrily. "Did you make any effort at all to keep him from finding out too much about us?"

Rynason shrugged. "I kept him pretty busy. All of the time I was running through Tebron's memories I could feel Horng screaming somewhere; he must have been too upset to do any probing in my mind."

Manning was silent for a moment. "Let's hope so," he said shortly. "If they find out how weak we are, how long it would take us to get reinforcements out here..."

"They're still just a dying race, remember," Rynason said. "They're not the Outsiders. What makes you so sure that they're dangerous?"

"Oh, come *on*, Lee! Think! They're in contact with the Outsiders; you said so yourself. And just remember this: *the Outsiders obviously considered it inevitable that there would be war between us.* Now put those two facts together and tell me the horses aren't dangerous!"

Rynason said slowly, "It isn't as simple as that. The order given to Tebron was to stop all scientific progress and stifle any military development, and he seems to have done just that. The idea was that if the Hirlaji were harmless when we found them there might be no need for fighting."

"Perhaps. But we weren't supposed to know that they were in contact with the Outsiders, either—that was probably part of the purpose of the block in the race-memory. But we got through the block, and they know it, and presumably by now the Outsiders know it. That changes the picture, and I'd like to know just how much it changes it."

"They're not in contact with the Outsiders any longer," said Rynason.

"What makes you so sure of that?"

"Tebron broke the contact—that was in the orders too. The priesthood, which had been the connecting link with the Outsiders through the machine, was disbanded. When Tebron died he didn't appoint a successor; the machine hasn't been used since."

Manning thought about that, still frowning. "Where is the machine?"

"I don't know. If it hasn't been kept in repair it might not even be usable any more, wherever it is."

"I'll tell you something, Lee," said Manning. "There's still too much that we don't know—and too much that the Hirlaji *do* know, now. Whether or not your horse-buddy was picking your brains, they know we're not as strong as they thought we were. It took us eight thousand years to get here instead of five thousand. Let's just hope they don't think about that too much."

He stopped, and paced to the window again. "Look around you, Lee—out on the street, in the town. We've hardly put our feet down on this planet; we've got very little in the way of weapons with us and it will take weeks to get any more in here; there's practically no organization here yet. We could be wiped off this planet before we knew what hit us. We're sitting ducks."

He came back to stand before Rynason. "And what about the Outsiders? They think of us strictly in terms of war, and they've been keeping themselves away from us all this time. That's obviously why they pulled out of this sector of space. Up until now we'd thought they were dead. But now we find they've been in contact with this planet ... all right, it was eight thousand years ago. But that's a lot more recent than the last evidences we've had of them, and they've obviously been watching us.

"Now, you've been in direct contact with the horses' minds; you've practically been one of them yourself, for awhile. All right, what's their reaction going to be when they realize that the Outsiders, their god, overestimated us? What will they do?"

Rynason thought about that. He tried to remember the minds he had touched during the linkage with Horng: Tebron, the ancient warrior-king, and the young Hirlaji staring at the buildings of one of the ancient cities, and the old, dying one who had decided not to plant again one year ... and Horng himself, tired and calm on the edge of the Flat, amid the ruins of a city. He remembered the others in that crumbling last home of an entire race...slow, quiet, uncaring.

"I don't think they'll do anything. They wouldn't see any point to it." He paused, remembering. "They lost all their purpose eight thousand years ago," he said quietly.

Manning grunted. "Somehow I lack your touching faith in them."

"And somehow," Rynason said, "I lack your burning ambition to find an enemy, a handy menace to crush. You argue too hard, Manning."

Manning raised an eyebrow. "I suppose I haven't even put a doubt in your mind about them? Not one doubt?"

Rynason turned away and didn't answer.

Manning sighed. "Maybe it's time I went out there myself and had a seance with the horses." He set down his glass of brandy, which he had been turning in his hand as he spoke. "Lee, I want you to check back here with me in two hours ... by then I should have things straightened up and ready to go."

He strode to the supply closet at one end of the room and took from it a belt and holster, from which he removed a recent-model regulation stunner. "This is as powerful a weapon as we have here so far, except for the heavy stuff. I hope we never have to use any of that—clearing it for use is a lot of red tape." He looked up and saw the cold expression on Rynason's face. "Of course, I hope we don't have to use the stunners, either," he said calmly.

Rynason turned without a word and went to the door. He stopped there for a moment and watched Manning checking over the weapon. He was thinking of the disintegrators he had seen on the steps of the Temple of Kor, and of the shell of a body tumbling out of the shadows.

"I'll see you at 600," he said.

CHAPTER SEVEN

Rynason spent the next two hours in town, moving through the windy streets and thinking about what Manning had said. He was right, in a way: this was no more than a foothold for the Earthmen, a touchdown point. It wasn't even a community yet; buildings were still going up, prices varied widely not only between landings of spacers but also according to who did the selling. A lot of the men here were trying some mining out on the west Flat; their findings had so far been small but they brought the only real income the planet had so far yielded. The rest of the town was rising on its own weight: bars, rooming houses, laundries, and diners—establishments which thrived only because there were men here to patronize them. Several weeks before a few of the men had tried killing and eating the small animals who darted through the alleys, but too many of those men had died and the practice had been quickly abandoned. And they had noticed that when those animals foraged in the refuse heaps outside the town, they died too.

A few of the big corporations had sent out field men to look around, but it was too soon for any industry to have established itself here; all the planet offered so far was room to expand. Despite the wide expansion of the Earthmen through the stars, a planet where conditions were at all favorable for living was not to be overlooked; the continuing population explosion, despite tight regulations on the inner worlds, had kept up with the colonization of these worlds, and new room was constantly needed.

But the planetfall on Hirlaj was still new. A handful of Earthmen had come, but they had not yet brought their civilization with them. They stood precariously on the Flat, waiting for more settlers to come in and build with them. If there should be trouble before more men arrived…

At 600 Rynason walked out on the dirt-packed street to Manning's quarters. He met Marc Stoworth and Jules Lessingham coming out the door. They looked worried.

"What's wrong?" he said.

They didn't stop as they went by. "Ask the old man," said Stoworth, going past with an uncharacteristically hurried step.

Rynason went on in through the open door. Manning was in the front room, amid several crates of stunner-units. He looked up quickly as Rynason entered and waved brusquely to him.

"Help me get this stuff unloaded, Lee."

Rynason fished for his sheath-knife and started cutting open one of the crates. "Why are you unloading the arsenal?"

"Because we may need it. Couple of the boys were just out at the horse-pasture, and they say the friendly natives have disappeared."

"Jules and Stoworth? I met them on the way in."

"They were doing some follow-up work out there … or at least they were going to. There's not a single one of them there, not a trace of them."

Rynason frowned. "They were all there this morning."

"They're not there now!" Manning snapped. "I don't like it, not after what you've told me. We're going to look for them."

"With stunners?"

"Yes. Right now Mara is out at the field clearing several of the fliers to use in scouting for them."

Rynason stacked the boxes of weapons and power-packs on the floor where Manning indicated. There were about forty of them—blunt-barrelled guns with thick casing around the powerpacks, weighing about ten pounds each. They looked as statically blunt as anvils, but they could stun any animal at two hundred yards; within a two-foot range, they could shake a rock wall down.

"How many men are we taking with us?" Rynason asked, eying the stacks on the floor.

Manning looked up at him briefly. "As many as we can get. I'm calling a militia; Stoworth and Lessingham went into town to round up some men."

So he was going ahead with the power-grab; Malhomme had been right. No danger had been proven yet, but that wouldn't stop Manning—nor the drifters he'd been buying in the town. Killing was an everyday thing to them.

"How many of the Hirlaji do you think we'll have to kill to make it look important to the Council?" Rynason asked after a moment, his voice deliberately inflectionless.

Manning looked up at him with a calculating eye. Rynason met his gaze directly, daring the man to take offense. He didn't.

"All right, it's a break for me," Manning shrugged. "What did you expect? There's precious little opportunity on this desert rock for leadership in any sense that you might approve of." He paused. "I don't know if it will be necessary to kill any of them. Take it easy and we'll see."

Rynason's eyes were cold. "All right, we'll see. But just remember, I'll be watching just as closely as you. If you start any violence that isn't necessary…"

"What will you do, Lee?" said Manning. "Report me to the Council? They'll listen to me before they'd pay attention to complaints from a nobody who's been drifting around the outworlds for most of his life. That's all you are, you know, Lee—a drifter, a bum, like the rest of them. That's what everybody out here on the Edge is … unless he does something about it.

"I hold the reins right now. If I decide to do something that you don't like, you won't be able to stop me…neither you, nor your female friend."

"So Mara's against you too?" Rynason said.

"She made a few remarks earlier," Manning said calmly. "She may regret it soon enough."

Rynason looked at the man through narrowed eyes for a moment, then strapped on a gunbelt and loaded one of the stunners. He snapped it into the holster carefully, wondering just what Manning had meant by his last remark. Was it a threat in any real sense, or was Manning just letting off steam? Well, they'd see about that too…and Rynason would be watching.

Within half an hour close to sixty men had collected outside Manning's door. They were dirty and unshaven; some of them were working in the town, a few were miners, but most of them were drifters who had followed the advance of the star frontier, who drank and brawled in the streets of the town, sleeping by day and raising hell at night. They stole when they could, killed when they wanted.

The drifters were men who had been all over the worlds of the Edge, who had spent years watching the new planets opened for colonization and exploitation, but had never got their own piece. They knew the feel of these planetfall towns on the Edge, and could talk for hours about the worlds they had seen. But they were city men, all of them; they had seen the untamed worlds, but only from the streets. They hadn't taken part in the exploring or the building, only in the initial touchdowns. When the building was done, they signed on to the spacers again and drifted to the next world, farther out.

Rynason looked at their faces from where he stood in the doorway, listening to Manning talking to them. They were hard men, mean and sometimes vicious. Nameless faces, all of them, having no place in the more developed areas of the Terran civilization. And maybe that was their own fault. But Rynason knew that they were running, not to anything, but from the civilization itself. Running... because when an area was settled and started to become respectable, they began to see what they did not have. The temporary quarters would come down, to be replaced by permanent buildings that were meant to be lived in, not just as places for sleeping. Closets, and shelters for landcars; quadsense receivers and food integrators. They didn't want to see that...because they hated it, or because they wanted it? It didn't matter, Rynason decided. They ran, and now they were here on the Edge with all their anger and frustration, and Manning was ready to give them a way to let it out.

At the side of the mob he saw a familiar grey shock of hair—Rene Malhomme. Was he with them, then? Rynason craned his neck for a better view, and for a moment the crowd parted enough to let him see Malhomme's face. He was looking directly toward Rynason, holding a dully gleaming knife flat against his thick chest … and his lips were drawn back into the crooked, sardonic smile which Rynason had seen many times. No, Malhomme at least was not part of this mob.

"We already know which direction they went," Manning was saying. "Lessingham will be in charge of the main body, and you'll follow him. If he gives you an order, *take it*. This is a serious business; we won't have room for bickering.

"Some of us will be scouting with the flyers. We'll be in radio contact with you. When we find out where they are we'll reconnoiter and make our plans from there."

Manning paused, looking appraisingly at the faces before him. "Most of you are armed already, I see. We have some extra stunners here; if you need them, come on up. But remember, the men who carry the shockers will be in front; and their business will be simply to down the horses—any killing that's to be done will be left to those of you who have knives, or anything lethal."

There was a rising wave of voices from the crowd. Some men came forward for weapons; Rynason saw others drawing knives and hatchets, and a few of them had heavy guns, projectile type. Rynason watched with narrowed eyes; it had been a filthy maneuver on Manning's part to organize this mob, and his open acceptance of their temper was dangerous. Once they were turned loose, what could stop them?

There was a sudden shouting in the back of the mob; men surged and fell away, cursing. Rynason heard scuffing back there, and sounds of bone meeting flesh. The men at the front of the mob turned to look back, and some tried to shove their way through to the fight.

A scream came from the midst of the crowd, and was answered by an excited, angry swelling of voices around the fighting men. Suddenly Manning was among them, smashing his way through with a stunner in his hand, swinging it like a club.

"Get the hell out of the way!" he shouted, stepping quickly through the men. They grumbled and fell back to let him by, but Rynason heard the men still fighting in the rear, and then he saw them. There were three of them, two men and what looked like a boy still in his teens. The boy had red hair and a dark, ruddy complexion: he was new to the outworlds. The two older men had the pallor of the Edge drifters, nurtured in the artificial light of spacers and sealed survival quarters on the less hospitable worlds.

The larger of the two men had a knife, a heavy blade of a type that was common out here; many of the men used them as hatchets when necessary. This one dripped with blood; the smaller man's left arm was torn open just below the shoulder, and hanging uselessly. He stood swaying in the dust, hurling a string of curses at the man with the knife, while the boy stood slightly behind him, staring with both fear and hatred in his eyes. He had a smaller knife, but he held it loosely and uncertainly at his side.

Manning stepped between them. He had sized up the situation already, and he paused now only long enough to bite out three short, clipped words which told these men exactly what he thought of them. The man with the knife stopped back and muttered something which Rynason didn't hear.

Manning raised the stunner coldly and let him have it. The blast caught the man in the shoulder and spun him around, throwing him into the crowd; several of them went down. The long knife fell to the ground, where dirt mixed with the blood on it. There was silence.

Manning looked around him, swinging the stunner loosely in his hand. After a moment he said calmly, but loud enough for all to hear, "We won't have time for fighting among ourselves. The next man who starts anything will be killed outright. Now get these men out of here." He turned and strode back through the mob while the boy and a couple of the other men took the wounded away.

Malhomme had moved further into the crowd. He was strangely silent; usually he went among these men roughly and jovially, cursing them all with goodnatured ease. But now he stood watching the men around him with a frown creasing his heavily lined face. Malhomme was worried, and Rynason, seeing that, felt his stomach tighten.

Manning faced the men from the front of the crowd. He stared at them shrewdly, holding each man's gaze for a few seconds. Then he grinned, and said, "Save it for the horses, boys. Save it for them."

Rynason rode out to the field with Manning, Stoworth, and a few of the others. It was a short trip in the landcar, and none of them spoke much. Even Stoworth rode silently, his usual easy flow of trivia forgotten. Rynason was thinking about Manning: he had handled the outbreak quickly and decisively enough, keeping the men in line, but it had been only a temporary measure. They would be expecting some real action soon, and Manning was already offering them the Hirlaji. If the alarm turned out to be a false one, would he be as easily able to stop them then?

Or would he even try?

The flyers were ready when they got to the field, but Mara was gone. Les Harcourt met them at the radio office on the edge of the field; he was the communications man out here. He led them into the low, quick-concrete construction office and shoved some forms at Manning to be signed.

"If there's any trouble, you'll be responsible for it," he said to Manning. "The men can look out for themselves, but the flyers are Company property."

Manning scowled impatiently and bent to sign the papers.

"Where's Mara?" Rynason asked.

"She's already taken one of the flyers out," Harcourt said. "Left ten minutes ago. We've got her screen in the next room." He waved a hand toward the door in the rear of the room.

Rynason went on back and found the live set. The screen, monitored from a camera on the flyer, showed the foothills of the southern mountains over which Mara was flying. They were bare and blunt; the rock outcroppings which thrust up from the Flat had been weathered smooth in the passage of years. Mara was passing over a low range and on to the desert beyond.

Rynason picked up the mike. "Mara, this is Lee; we just got here. Have you found them yet?"

Her voice came thinly over the speaker. "Not yet. I thought I saw some movement in one of the passes, but the light wasn't too good. I'm looking for that pass again."

"All right. We'll be going up ourselves in a few minutes; if you find them, be careful. Wait for us."

He refitted the mike in its stand and rose. But as he turned to the door her voice came again: "There they are!"

He looked at the screen, but for the moment he couldn't see anything. Mara's flyer was coming down out of the rocky hills now, the Flat stretching before her on the screen. Rynason could see the pass through which she had been flying, but there was no movement there; it took him several seconds to see the low ruins off to the right, and the figures moving through them.

The screen banked and turned toward them; she was lowering her altitude.

"I see them," he said into the mike. "Can't make out what they're doing, on the screen. Can you see them any more clearly?"

"They're entering one of the buildings down there," she said after a moment. "I've counted almost twenty of them so far; they must all be here."

"Can you go down and see what they're doing? The sooner we find out, the better: Manning's got a pretty ugly bunch of so-called vigilantes on the way out there."

She didn't reply, but on the screen he saw the crumbling buildings grow larger and nearer. He could make out individual structures now: a wall had fallen and was half-buried in the dust and sand; an entire roof had caved in on another building, leaving only rubble in the interior. It was difficult to tell sometimes when the original lines of the buildings had fallen: they had all been smoothed by the wind-blown sand, so that broken pillars looked almost as though they had been built that way, smooth and upright, solitary.

At last, he saw the Hirlaji. They were slowly mounting the steps of one of the largest of the buildings and passing into the shadows of the interior. This building was not as deteriorated as most of the others; as Mara's flyer dipped low over it Rynason could see its characteristic lines unbroken and clear.

With a start, he sat up and said hurriedly, "Mara, take another close pass over that building, the one they're entering."

In a moment she came in again over the smooth stone structure, and Rynason looked closely at the screen. There was no mistaking it now: the high steep steps leading up to a colonnade which almost circled the building, the large carvings over the main entrance.

"You'd better set down away from them!" he said. "That's the Temple of Kor!" But even as he finished speaking the image on the screen jolted and rocked, and the flyer dipped even closer toward the jumbled ruins below.

"They're firing something!"

He saw that she was trying to gain altitude, but something was wrong; the buildings on the screen dipped and wavered, up and down, spinning.

"Mara! Pull up—get out of there!"

"One of the wings is damaged," she said quickly, and suddenly there was another jolt on the screen and he heard her gasp. The picture spun and righted itself, seemed to hang motionless for a moment, and then the stone wall of one of the buildings was directly ahead and growing larger.

"Mara!"

The image spun wildly, the building filled the screen, and then it went black; he heard a crash from the speaker, cut off almost before it had sounded. The room was silent.

CHAPTER EIGHT

Rynason stared at the dead screen for only a moment; he wheeled and ran back to the outer room.

"Let's get those flyers up! Mara's found them, but they've brought her down." He was already going out the door as he spoke.

Manning and the others were right behind him as he dashed out onto the field. Rynason headed for the nearest flyer, a small runabout which had been discarded as obsolete on the inner worlds and consigned to use out here on the Edge, where equipment was scarce. He leaped through the port and was shutting the door when Manning caught it.

"Where are they? What's happened to the woman?"

"They were shooting something!" Rynason snapped. The knife-scar over his right eye stood out sharply in his anger. "She crashed—may be badly hurt. She didn't have too much altitude, though. The hell with where she is— *follow* me!"

He slammed the door and squeezed into the flying seat. While he warmed the engines he saw the others scattering across the field to the other flyers. In a moment the hum of the radioset told him that their communications were open. He saw the props of the other flyers starting to turn, and flicked on his mike.

"They're on the other side of the south range," he said quickly. "She didn't give me coördinates, but I should be able to find the spot. When we get there, we land away from the city and go in on foot."

Manning's voice came coldly through the radioset: "Are you giving orders now, Lee?"

"Right now I am, yes! If you want to try going in before reconnoitering, that's your funeral. They have weapons."

"When we touch ground again I'll take over," Manning said. "Now let's get going—Lee, you're first."

But Rynason was already starting his run across the field. When he had some speed he kicked in the rocket booster and fought the little flyer skyward. When he had caught the air he banked southward and fed the motors all he had. He didn't look around for the others; he was setting his own pace.

The mountain range was ten miles to the south; they should be able to make it in five or six minutes, he figured. Below him on the dry Flat he saw the pale shadow of his flyer skimming across the dust. The drone of the motors filled the compartment.

The radio cut in again. It was Manning. "What's this about a city, Lee? Is that where they are?"

"The City of the Temple," Rynason said. "It's down among overhanging rocks—no wonder we hadn't seen it before. Doesn't seem to have been used for centuries or more. But that's where the Temple of Kor is—and the Hirlaji are all in the Temple."

Static hissed at him for a moment. "How did they bring her down?" someone asked. It sounded like Stoworth.

"Probably the disintegrators," Rynason said. "The Hirlaji don't have many of them, but they've got enough power to give us a lot of trouble."

"And they're using them, eh?" Manning said. "What do you think of your horses now, Lee?"

Rynason didn't answer.

In a few minutes they were over the range. Rynason had to scout for awhile before he found the pass he had seen on Mara's screen, but once he saw it below him he followed it out to the other side. The city was there, lying darkly amid the shadows of the mountains. Rynason banked off and set down half a mile away.

He waited for the others to land before he left the flyer. He took a pair of binocs from the supply kit and trained them on the city across the Flat, but he couldn't find Mara's fallen flyer.

When they were all down he clambered out of the compartment and alighted heavily in the dust. Manning strode quickly to him, wearing twin stunners. He took one from its holster and fingered it thoughtfully as he spoke.

"The main party was back in the pass. They should be here inside half an hour. We'll storm the temple immediately—we've got them outnumbered."

Rynason made a dubious sound deep in his throat, looking out at the city. He was remembering that he had seen it before from this Flat…and had stormed it before. The defensive walls were high.

"They can fire down on us from the walls," he said in a low voice. "There's no cover out there—they'd wipe half of us out before we could get in."

"We can come around from the pass," Manning said. "There's plenty of cover from that direction."

"And more fortification, too!" Rynason snapped. "Just remember, Manning, that city was built as a fortress. We'd *have* to come from the Flat."

Manning paused, frowning. "We've got to take them anyway," he said slowly. "Damn it, we can't just stand here and wait for them to come out at us. What are they doing, anyway?"

Rynason regarded the older man for several moments, almost amused. "Right now," he said, "they're probably having a conference—with the Outsiders. That's where the machine is, remember."

"Then the sooner we attack, the better," Manning said. "Marc, get the main party on the hand-radio—tell them to get here as fast as they can." He turned for a moment to look out across the Flat at the city. "And you can promise them some action," he said.

Stoworth dropped the radio from his shoulder and threw back the cover. He switched on the power, and static sounded in the dry air. He lifted the mike ... and a voice cut through the static.

"Is anyone picking this up? Is anyone there?"

It was Mara's voice.

Rynason knelt beside the set and took the mike from Stoworth's hand. "This is Lee. Are you hurt?"

"Lee?"

"I hear you. Are you hurt?"

"Not badly. Lee, what are you doing? I saw the flyers land."

"Manning wants to attack the city as soon as the land party gets here. What's going on there?"

"I'm ... in the temple. I've been trying to communicate with them. I've got an interpreter, but they don't listen to what I say. Lee, this is incredible here! They've brought out a lot of weapons...some of them don't work. The hall is half-filled with dust and sand, and they move so clumsily! They're trying to hurry, because they saw you too, but it's like ... like they've forgotten how. They think they can get rid of us all, but they... It's pitiful—they're so slow."

"Those disintegrators aren't slow," Rynason said. Manning was standing beside him; he dropped a hand on his shoulder, but Rynason shook it off. "Are they using the machine … the altar?"

"They were using it when they brought me in. I think it *is* the Outsiders. But they don't seem to know it's just a machine—they kneel in front of it, and chant. It's so strange, in that language of theirs…those thin, high voices, and the echoes…"

"They're holding you prisoner?"

"Yes. I think they want to hold you off till they can get ready for their own attack."

"*For their what?*" Rynason stood up, and looked toward the city; he could see no movement there.

"I know…it's incredible. Lee, they don't know what they're doing. Horng said on the interpreter that they were going to drive us off the planet, and then rebuild their cities, and re-arm. It's something to do with Kor, or the Outsiders. The orders have changed. They think that if they can drive us away for awhile they can build themselves up to where they can repel any further touchdowns here."

"This order came from the machine?"

"Yes. There was a mistake, and Horng realized it after you linked with him this morning. The Outsiders, or Kor or whatever it is, had overestimated us."

"Maybe then, but not now. They're committing suicide!" Rynason said.

"I know, and I tried to tell them that. But the machine says differently. Lee, do you think that's really the Outsiders?"

"If it is," he said slowly, "they wouldn't send the Hirlaji against us without some help." He thought a minute, while the wind of the Flat blew sand against his leg and static came from the radio. "They could be making another mistake!" Mara said. "I'm sure what they told the

Outsiders wasn't true—they think they're as strong as they were before. But their eyes...their eyes are afraid. I know it."

"Do they know what you're saying to me?"

"No. Lee, I'm not even sure they know what a radio is. Maybe they think I carry my portable altar with me." Her voice had taken on a frantic note. "It's a ... a simple case of freedom of religion, Lee! Freedom of religion!"

"Mara! Calm down! Calm down!" He waited for a few seconds, until her voice came again, more quietly:

"I'm sorry...it's just that they're so..."

"Forget it. Sit tight there. I think I know how to slip in—alone." He switched off.

He stood up and shrugged his shoulders heavily, loosening his tensed muscles. Then he turned purposefully to Manning.

"The rest of the party won't be here for awhile yet, so you can't possibly go in now. I'm going to try to get Mara out before any fighting starts."

"What if they capture you too?" Manning said. "I can't hold off an attack too long—you could be right about the Outsiders helping them. The sooner we finish them off, the better."

Rynason looked coldly at him. "You heard what Mara said. We won't have any trouble taking them. You can't attack them while she's in there, though. Or can you?"

"Lee. I've told you—I can't take chances. If the Outsiders are in this, it's a dangerous business. You can go in if you want, but we're not waiting more than half an hour for you to get out."

Rynason met his gaze steadily for a moment, then nodded brusquely. "All right." He turned and moved into the over-hanging shadows of the mountains, toward the ancient, alien city.

He stayed in the shadows as he approached the walls of the fortress, darting quickly across exposed ground. The Hirlaji were large and powerful, physical battle with them was of course out of the question. But he had some things on his side: he was small, and therefore less likely to be seen; he was faster than the quiet, aged aliens. And he knew the city, the fortress and the temple, almost as well as they did.

Perhaps better, in fact, for his purposes. For while he had shared Tebron's mind he had been...not only Tebron, but also Rynason, Earthman. A corner of his mind had been alert and aware...hearing the distant screams of Horng, wondering about the design of the Altar of Kor. And he had seen other things when he looked through Tebron's eyes: when the ancient warlord had stormed the city-fortress, there had been an observer in him who had said: An Earthman could go in this way, unobserved. A smaller attacker could slip through *here*, could conceal himself where no Hirlaji could reach.

He arrived, at last, at the base of the wall where the blunt rocks of the mountains tumbled to a dead-end against flat, weathered stone. So far he must not have been seen; there had been no disintegrator beams fired at him, no leathery Hirlaji heads watching from the walls. He flattened against the stone and raised his eyes to the barriers.

The wall here had been built higher than the portions which faced the Flat, and it was stronger. No one had tried to storm the city from this position, because it was too well protected. But the walls had been built against the heavy, clumsy bodies of the grey aliens; with luck, a man could scale this wall. The footholds in the weathered stones would be precarious, but perhaps it could be done. And the Hirlaji, who regarded this wall as impregnable, would not be guarding it.

Sighting upward from flat against the wall, he chose his path quickly, and began to climb. The stone was smooth but grainy; he dug his fingers into narrow niches and pulled himself slowly upward, bracing himself with footholds whenever he could. It was laborious, painful work; twice he lost handholds and hung precariously until his straining fingers again found some indentation. Sweat covered him; the wind from the Flat whipped around the wall and touched the moisture on his back coldly. But his face was set in a frozen grimness and though his breath came in gasps he made no other sound.

When he had neared the top he suddenly seemed to reach a dead-end; the stones were smooth above him. His arms ached, his shoulders seemed deadened; he clung numbly to the wall and searched for another path. When he found it, he had to descend ten feet and move to the right before he could re-ascend; as he retraced his route down the wall he noticed blood where his torn fingers had left their mark. But he could not feel the pain in his fingers.

At last, when the wall had come to seem a separate world of existence which was all that he would ever know, a vertical plane to which he clung with dim determination, hardly knowing why any longer … at last, he reached the top. His groping hand reached up and found the edge of the wall; his fingers grasped it gratefully and he pulled himself up to hang by both hands and survey the interior of the fortress.

A deserted floor stretched before him, shadowed by the late-afternoon darkness which crept down from the mountains to rest on the aged remains of the city. Forty feet down the walkway he saw stairs descending, but his head swam and all he could focus on clearly was the light film of dust and sand which covered even this topmost level of the city, blown in shallow drifts against the walls which rose a few feet above the floor here. There were no footprints in that dust; no one had walked here for thousands of years.

Wearily, he pulled himself over the last barrier and fell numbly to the floor, where he lay for long minutes fighting for breath. His lungs were raw; the thin air of the planet caught and rasped in his throat. His hands were torn and bleeding, and the knife-scar over his right eye had begun to throb, but he ignored the pain. He had to clear his head....

Eventually he was able to stand, swaying beneath the dark sky. Below him he saw the city, broken and dim, empty streets winding between fallen walls and pillars. Mara's flyer lay shattered against one of those broken walls; seeing it, he wondered how badly she had been hurt.

He moved toward the stairs, and descended them slowly. The stairs of the city were as he had remembered them from Tebron's memories, and yet not the same. To the Earthman they were steep: the steps were like separate levels, three feet across and almost four feet deep. His legs ached at each step as the shock of his weight fell on them.

He reached the bottom level and paused in the doorway onto the street. It was empty, but he had to think a moment before he could remember his bearings. Yes, the Temple was that way, somewhere down the dusty street. He moved through the deeper shadows at the base of the buildings, remembering.

Tebron had taken this city at the head of a force of warriors. To him it had been large and majestic, a place of power and knowledge. But Rynason, moving wearily through the dust of the ages which had fallen upon the city since the ancient king, found it not merely large, but huge; not majestic, but futile. And the power and knowledge which it once had held was but a dusty shadow now. Somewhere ahead, in the Temple, the survivors of that ages-old culture were trying to bring the city to life again. With or without the Outsiders, he felt, they must fail. They really wanted to bring themselves back to life, to reawaken their minds, their dreams, their own power. But they tried to do it with memories, and that was not the way.

No one was guarding the Temple. Rynason went up the steps as quickly as he could, vaulting from level to level, trying to stay in the shadows, listening for movement. But sounds did not carry far in the air of Hirlaj; the aliens would not hear him approaching, but he might not hear any of them either until he stumbled upon them.

At the top of the stairs he darted into the shadows of the colonnade which surrounded the interior. Doorways opened at intervals of fifty feet around the building; he would have to circle to the side and enter there if at all. He slipped quickly between the columns and paused at the third doorway. He dropped to the floor, lay flat on his chest and looked inside.

They were all there—two dozen heavy grey aliens, sitting, standing, staring quietly at the floor. There was little movement among them, but nevertheless he could feel the excitement which pervaded the Temple. No, not excitement—anxiety. Fear. Watching those huge bodies huddling into themselves, he heard an echo of Horng's screams in his mind. These creatures were afraid of battle, of conflict, and yet they had thrust themselves into a fight which they must lose. Did they know that? Could they believe what the machine of the Outsiders told them, after it had been proven fallible?

The Eye of Kor glowed dully in the dark inner room; two of the Hirlaji stood silently before it, watching, waiting. But the religion of Kor had played no part in the lives of the Hirlaji for generations. Now that the ancient, muddled religion had been brought to life again, could it have the same hold on them that it had once had?

Mara was on the floor of the Temple, leaning with her back against the wall. One of the doorways from the outer colonnade was nearby, but five of the Hirlaji surrounded her. And with a start Rynason noticed that her left arm hung limp and twisted at her side, and blood showed on her forehead. Her face showed no emotion, but as he watched she raised her right hand to run fingers through her long dark hair, nervously.

She had not seen him, but she was waiting. When he made his move she would follow him. Rynason slipped back from the doorway and circled the building again until he had reached the entrance nearest the girl. He drew out his stunner from its holster and looked at it for a moment. He would have to be fast; his weapon would give him no advantage against the disintegrators of the Hirlaji, but surprise and speed might. And, perhaps ... fear.

He broke around the corner of the doorway at a dead run, firing as he went. Two of the Hirlaji fell before they could even turn; they crumpled to the floor heavily. Then he screamed—a high scream, like Horng's, and as loud as he could make it, a wail, a cry of anguish and terror and pain. They felt it, and it touched a response in them; the Hirlaji who surrounded Mara twisted to look at him, but they instinctively shrank away. He continued to fire, bringing down three more of them while the confusion lasted. He broke through to Mara, who was already on her feet; without breaking his stride he grasped her by her good shoulder and pulled her along with him as he ran through.

But some of the Hirlaji recovered in time to block their escape. Rynason wheeled, looking frantically around the room for an unguarded exit. None of those within reach were clear. He fired again, and ran for the altar.

One of the Hirlaji had raised a disintegrator; Rynason caught him with the stunner as he fired, and the beam of the alien's weapon shot past his leg, digging a pit into the floor beyond him. Other weapons were raised now; they had only seconds left.

But they had reached the altar; the two Hirlaji there moved to block them, but they were unarmed and Rynason dropped them with the stunner. He pushed Mara past them and around to the side of the altar, seeking cover from the disintegrators.

Behind the altar, there was a space just large enough for them to squeeze through. Rynason's heart leaped; he pointed quickly to it and turned to fire again as Mara pushed her way into the narrow aperture. A disintegrator beam hissed over his head; another tore into the wall two feet away from him. The Hirlaji were trying to keep their fire away from the altar itself.

Rynason turned and squeezed behind the altar as soon as Mara was clear. It was tight, but he made it, and once through the narrow opening they found more room in the darkness. They could hear noise outside as the Hirlaji moved toward the altar, but it sounded far away and dim. Mara moved back into the darkness, and he followed.

They moved perhaps twenty feet into the wall behind the altar before they were brought to a halt. The passage ended. Well, no matter; if it was not an escape route, at least it would afford cover from the weapons of the Hirlaji. Rynason dropped to the floor and rested.

Mara sat beside him. "Lee, you shouldn't have tried it," she said anxiously. "Now we're trapped." He felt her hand touch his face in the darkness.

"Maybe," he said. "But we may be able to catch them off their guard again, and if so we may be able to get out."

She was silent. He felt her lean against his shoulder wearily, her hair soft against his neck. Then he remembered that she had been hurt.

"What happened to your arm? And you were bleeding."

"I think it's broken. The bleeding was nothing, though: you should see yourself. You were so tattered and bloody when you came in that I hardly knew you. Knights should come in more properly shining armor."

He grinned wearily. "Wait till next time."

"Lee, where are we?" she said abruptly. Their eyes were becoming adjusted to the darkness, and they could see rising around them a complexity of machine relays, connectives, and pieces which did not seem to make sense.

Rynason looked a little more closely at the complex. It was definitely Outsiders work, but what was it? Part of the Altar of Kor, most obviously, but the Outsiders telecommunicators had never before used such extensive machinery. Yet it did look familiar. He tried to remember the different types of Outsiders machinery that had been found and partially then reconstructed by the advancing Earthmen in the centuries in the past. There weren't many....

Then, suddenly, he had it, and it was so simple that he was surprised he hadn't thought of it before.

"This is Kor," he said. "It's not a communicator—it's a computer. An Outsiders computer."

CHAPTER NINE

Mara's frown deepened; she looked around them in the dimness, her eyes taking in the complexity and extent of the circuitry. It faded into the darkness behind them; lines ran into the walls and floor.

"They built their computers in the grand manner, didn't they?" she said softly.

"I've seen fragments of them before," Rynason said. "This is a big one—no telling how much area the total complex takes up. One thing's certain, though: it's no ordinary computer of theirs. Not for plain math-work, nor even for specialized computations, like the one on Rigel II—that was apparently used for astrogation, but it wasn't half the size of this. And navigation between stars, even with the kind of drive they must have had, is no simple problem."

"The Hirlaji think it's a god," she said.

"That raised another problem," Rynason mused. "The Outsiders built it, and must have left it here when they pulled back to wherever they were going...if they ever left the planet. But the Hirlaji use it, and they communicate with it verbally. The Hirlaji are apparently responsible for keeping it protected since then. But why should the Hirlaji be able to use it?"

"Unless they're the Outsiders after all?" said Mara.

Rynason frowned. "No, I'm still not convinced of that. The clue seems to be that they communicate verbally with it—they must have been using it since before they developed telepathy."

"Couldn't there have been direct contact between the Hirlaji and the Outsiders back when the Hirlaji were just evolving out of the beast stage?"

"There must have been," said Rynason. "The Temple rituals are conducted in an even older form of their language than most remembered—a proto-language that was kept alive only by the priest caste, because the machine had been set to respond to that language."

"But aren't primitive languages usually composed of simple, basic words and concepts? How well could they communicate in such a language?"

"Not very well," Rynason said. "Which would explain why the machine seemed to make mistakes—clumsiness of language. So the Outsiders, maybe, left the machine when they pulled out, but they set it to respond to the Hirlaji language because our horsefaced friends were beginning to build a civilization of their own and the Outsiders thought they'd leave them some guidance...." He stopped for a moment, remembering that first linkage with Horng, and Tebron's memories. "The Hirlaji called them the Old Ones," he said.

"And that order to Tebron...about the other race that they would meet someday. That was based on Outsiders observations."

"I wonder when the Outsiders were on Earth," Rynason said. "Sometime after we'd started our own rise, certainly. Maybe in ancient Mesopotamia, or India. Or later, during the Renaissance?"

"The time doesn't matter, does it?" Mara said. "They touched down on Earth, took note of us, and left. Somehow they thought we were going to develop more rapidly than we did."

"Probably before the Dark Ages," Rynason said. "Maybe they didn't see that thousand-year setback coming..." He stopped, and stood up in the low passageway among the ancient circuitry. "So here we are, second-guessing the Outsiders. And outside, their proteges have disintegrators probably left by the Outsiders, and they're just waiting for us to try to get out."

"Our new-found knowledge isn't doing us much good, is it?" she said.

He shook his head slowly. "When I was still on the secondary senseteach units I met Rene Malhomme for the first time. My father worked the spacers, so I don't even remember what planet this was on. But I remember the night I first saw Rene—he was speaking from the top of a blue-lumber pile, shouting about the corporations that were moving in. He was getting all worked up about something, and several people in the crowd were shouting back at him; I stopped to watch. All of a sudden six or seven men moved in from somewhere and dragged him down from where he was standing. There was a fight— people were thrown all around. I hid till it was over.

"When the crowd finally cleared, there was Rene. His clothes were torn, but he wasn't hurt. Every one of the men who had attacked him had to be carried away; I think one of them was dead. Rene stood there laughing; then he saw me hidden in the darkness and he took me home. He told me that when he'd been younger he'd worked his way all the way in to Earth, and studied some of the cultures there. He'd learned karate, which was an ancient Japanese way of fighting."

Rynason took a deep breath. "He said everything a person learns will be useful someday. And I believed him."

"A nice parable," Mara said. "We could use him against the Hirlaji, though."

Rynason was silent, thinking. If they could only catch the aliens off guard...but of course they couldn't, now. He let his eyes wander aimlessly along the circuitry surrounding them. Tell me, old Kor, what do we do now?

After a moment his eyes narrowed; he reached up and traced a connection with his fingers, back to the front, toward the altar. It led directly to...the speaker!

The voice of Kor.

And if he could interrupt that connection, put his own voice through the speaker, out through the altar....

"Mara, we're going out. I've found my own brand of karate for our friends out there."

He helped her to her feet. She moved somewhat painfully, her broken left arm hanging stiffly at her side, but she made no protest.

"We've got to be fast," he said. "I don't know how well this will work—it depends on how much they trust their clay-footed god today." Quickly, he outlined his plan. Mara listened silently and nodded.

Then he set to work. It was largely guesswork, following those intricate alien connections, but Rynason had seen this part of such machines before. He found the penultimate point at which the impulses from the brain were translated into sound and broadcast through the speaker. He disconnected this, his torn fingers working awkwardly on the delicate linkages.

"Ready?"

Mara was just inside the narrow passage behind the altar. She nodded quickly.

Rynason twisted himself so that he could speak directly into the input of the speaker. He raised his voice to approximate the thin, high sounds of the Hirlaji language.

Remain motionless. Remain motionless. Remain motionless.

The command burst out upon the altar room of the Temple, shattering the silence. The Hirlaji turned in surprise to the altar—and stood still.

Remain motionless. Remain motionless.

It was the phrase he had heard the machine use so often to Tebron, king priest leader of all Hirlaj. It had meant something else then, but the proto-language of the Hirlaji had no precise meanings; given by itself, it seemed to mean precisely what it said.

"All right, let's go out!" Rynason said, and the two of them broke from behind the altar. The Hirlaji stood completely still; several of those that Rynason had dropped with his stunner had recovered consciousness, but they made no move either. Rynason and the girl ran right through the quiet aliens; only a few of them turned shadowed eyes to look at them as they passed. They made the outside colonnade in safety, and paused there.

"They may see through this in a minute," Rynason said. "Don't wait for me—get out of the city!"

"You're not coming?"

"I won't be too far behind. Get going!"

She hesitated only a moment, then hurried down the broad levels of the Temple steps. Rynason watched her to the bottom, then turned and re-entered the altar room.

Rynason went quickly among them, taking their weapons. Most of them made no effort to stop him, but a few tightened their grips on the disintegrators and he had to pry those thick fingers from the weapons, cursing to himself. How long would they wait?

There were fourteen of the disintegrators. They were large and heavy; he couldn't hold them all at once. He dumped five of them outside the altar room and returned to disarm the rest of the aliens. Sweat formed beads on his forehead, but he moved without hesitation.

Another of the Hirlaji tightened his grip when Rynason began to take the weapon from him. He looked up, and saw the quiet eyes of Horng resting on him. The leathery grey wrinkles which surrounded those eyes quivered slightly, but otherwise he made no movement. Rynason dropped his gaze from that contact and wrested the weapon away.

As he started to move on to the next, Horng silently dipped his massive head to one side. Rynason felt a chill go down his back.

In a few more minutes he had disarmed them all. He set the last three disintegrators on the stone floor of the colonnade—and a movement in the distance caught his eye. It was on the south wall of the city; two men stood for a moment silhouetted against the Flat, then disappeared into the shadows. In a moment, another man appeared, and he too dropped inside the wall.

So Manning had already sent the men in. The mob was unleashed.

Rynason hesitated for a moment or two, then turned and went quickly back into the altar room. Mara's radio was there; he lifted it by its strap and took it with him out to the colonnade.

He could see the Earthmen moving through the streets now, darting from wall to wall in the gathering darkness of evening. In a short time it would be full night—and Rynason knew that these men would like nothing better than to attack in the dark.

He warmed the radio and opened the transmitter.

"Manning, call off your dogs. I've disarmed the Hirlaji."

The radio spat static at him, and for several seconds he thought his signal hadn't even been picked up. But at last there was a reply:

"Then get out of the Temple. It's too late to stop this."

"Manning!"

"I said get clear. You've done all you can there."

"Damn it, there's no need for any fighting!"

Manning's voice sounded cold even in the faint reception of the hand-radio. "That's for me to decide. I'm running this show, remember."

"You're running a massacre!" Rynason shouted.

"Call it what you like. Mara says they weren't so docile when you broke in."

Rynason's mind raced; he had to stall for time. If he could get Manning to stop those men until they cooled down...

"Manning, there's no need for this! Didn't she tell you that the altar is just a computer? These people haven't had anything to do with the Outsiders since before they can remember!"

The radio carried the faint sound of Manning's chuckle. "So now they're people to you, Lee? Or are you one of them now?"

"What the hell are you talking about?"

"Lee, my boy, you're sounding like an old horsefaced nursemaid. You linked minds with them, and you say you were practically a Hirlaji yourself when you went into that linkage. Well, I'm not so sure you ever came out of it. You're *still* one of them!"

"Is that the only reason you can think of that I might have for wanting to prevent a massacre?" Rynason said icily.

"If they tried to revolt once, they'll try it again," Manning said. "Well crush them *now*."

"You think that will impress the Council? Slaughtering the only intelligent race we've found?"

"I'm not playing to the Council!" Manning snapped. "I've got these men following me, and I'll listen to what *they* want!"

Rynason stared hard at the microphone for a few moments. "Are you sure you aren't afraid of your own mob?" he said.

"We're coming in, Lee. Get out of there or we'll cut you down too."

"Manning!"

"I'm switching off."

"*Not quite yet.* There's one more thing, and you'd better hear this one!"

"Make it fast," Manning said. His voice sounded uninterested.

"If any of your boys try to come in, I'll stop them myself. I've got the disintegrators, and I'll use them."

There was silence from the radio, save for the static. It lasted for long seconds. Then:

"It's your funeral." There was a faint click as Manning switched off.

Rynason stared angrily at the radioset for a moment, then left it lying at the top of the steps and went back inside. The Hirlaji stood motionlessly in dimness; it took awhile for Rynason's eyes to adjust to it. He found the interpreter that Mara had left and quickly hooked it up to

Horng. The alien's eyes, moving heavily in their sockets, watched him as he connected the wires.

When everything was ready Rynason lifted the interpreter's mike. "The Earthmen are going to attack you," he said. "I want to help you fight them off."

There was no reaction from the alien; only those quiet eyes resting on him like the shadows of the entire past.

"Can you still believe that Kor is a god? That's only a machine—I spoke through it myself, minutes ago! Don't you realize that?"

After a moment Horng's eyes slowly closed and opened in acknowledgement. KOR WAS GOD KNOWLEDGE. THE OLD ONES DIED BEFORE TIME, AND PASSED INTO KOR. NOW KOR IS DEAD.

"And all of you will be dead too!" Rynason said.

The huge alien sat unmoving. His eyes turned away from Rynason.

"You've got to fight them!" Rynason said.

But he could see that it was useless. Horng had made no reply, but Rynason knew what was in his thoughts now. THERE IS NO PURPOSE.

CHAPTER TEN

Wearily, Rynason switched off the interpreter, leaving the wires still connected to the alien. He walked through the faintly echoing, dust-filled temple and stepped out onto the colonnade around it. It was almost dark now; the deep blue of the Hirlaj sky had turned almost black and the pinpoint lights of the stars broke through. The wind was rising from the Flat; it caught his hair and whipped it roughly around his head. He looked up at the emerging stars, remembering the day when Horng had suddenly, inexplicably stood and walked to the base of a broken staircase. He had looked up those stairs, past where they had broken and fallen, past the shattered roof, to the sky. The Hirlaji had never reached the stars, but they might have. It had taken a god, or a jumbled legacy from an older, greater race, to forestall them. And now all they had was the dust and the wind.

Rynason could hear the rising moan of that wind gathering itself around him, building to a wailing planet-dirge among the columns of the Temple. And inside, the Hirlaji were dying. The knives and bludgeons of the Earth mob outside would only complete the job; the Hirlaji were too tired to live. They dreamed dimly under the shadowed foreheads…dreamed of the past. And sometimes, perhaps, of the stars.

Behind the altar, the huge and intricate mass of alien circuits glowed and clicked and pulsated…slowly; seemingly at random, but steadily. The brain must be self-perpetuating to have lasted this long … feeding its energy cells from some power-source Rynason could only guess at, and repairing its time-worn linkages when necessary. In its memory banks was stored the science of the race which had preceded even the ancient Hirlaji. The Outsiders had sprung up when this planet was young, had fought their way to the stars and galaxies, and eventually, when aeons of time pressed down, had pulled in their outposts and fallen back to this world. And they had died here, on this world, falling to dust which was ground under by the grey race which had followed them to dominance. "Before time," Horng had said; that must have meant before the Hirlaji had developed telepathy, before the period covered by the race-memory.

But the Outsiders were still here, alive in that huge alien brain ... the science, the knowledge, the strange arts of a race which had conquered the stars while men still wondered about the magic of lightning and fire. A science was encapsuled here which could speak of war and curiosity as discontent, but could say nothing definite of contentment. An incomplete science? A merely alien science? Rynason didn't know.

And the Hirlaji... Twenty-six of their race remained, dreaming under heavy domes through which the stars shone at night and silhouetted the worn edges of broken stone. Twenty-six grey, hopeless beings who had not even been waiting. And the Earthmen had come.

For a moment Rynason wondered if the Hirlaji did not perhaps carry a message for the Earthmen too: that decadence was the price of peace, death the inevitable end of contentment. The Hirlaji had stilled themselves, back in the grey past ... had taken their measure of quiet and contentment for thousands of years, the searching drives of their race dying within them. And this was their end.

THERE IS NO PURPOSE.

Rynason shook himself, and felt the cold wind cut through his clothing; it reawakened him. Stooping, he gathered up several of the disintegrators and brought them with him to the head of the massive stairs up which the attackers must come. He crouched beside those stairs, watching for movement below. But he couldn't see anything.

Something about the Hirlaji still bothered him; kneeling in the gathering darkness he finally isolated it in his mind. It was their hopelessness, the numbness that had crept over them through the centuries. No purpose? But they had lived in peace for thousands of years. No, their death was not merely one of decadence…it was suffocation.

They had not chosen peace; it had been thrust upon them. The Hirlaji had been at the height of their power, their growth still gathering momentum…and they had to stifle it. The end in view didn't really matter: it had not been what they would have chosen. And, having had peace forced upon them before they had been ready for it, they had been unable to enjoy it; and the stifling of scientific curiosity that had been necessary to complete the suppression of the war-instinct had left the Hirlaji with nothing.

But it had all been so unnecessary, Rynason thought. The ancient Outsiders brain, computing from insufficient evidence probably gathered during a brief touchdown on Earth, had undoubtedly been able to give only a tentative appraisal of the situation. But the proto-Hirlaji language was not constructed to accommodate if's and maybe's, and the judgments of the brain were taken as law by the Hirlaji.

Now the Earthmen for whom this race had deadened itself into near-extinction would complete the job... because the Hirlaji had learned their mistake far too late.

Rynason shook his head; there was a sickness in his stomach, a gnawing anger at the ways of history. It was capricious, cruel, senseless. It played jokes spanning millennia.

Suddenly there were sounds on the stairs below him. Rynason's head jerked up and he saw five of the Earthmen climbing the stairs, moving as quickly as they could from level to level, crouching momentarily at each beneath the cover of the steps. He raised one of the disintegrators, feeling the rage building up within him.

There was a humming sound by his ear; the beam of one of the stunners passed by him, touching the rock wall. The wall vibrated at the touch, but the range was too great for the beam to have done it any damage. They were close enough, though to stun Rynason if they hit him.

He dropped flat, looking for the man who had fired. In a moment he found him: a small, lean man slipped almost silently over the edge of one of the step-levels and rolled quickly to cover beneath the next. He had got further than Rynason had realized; only three levels separated them now. He could see, from this distance in the near-dark, the cruel lines of the man's face. It was a harsh, dirty face, with wrinkles like seams; the man's eyes were harsh slits. Rynason had seen too many faces like that here on the Edge; this was a man with a bitter hatred, looking for the chance to unleash it upon anyone who got in his way. And the enjoyment which Rynason saw gleaming in the man's eyes chilled him momentarily.

In that moment the man leaped to the next level, sending off a beam which struck the wall two feet from

Rynason; he felt the stinging vibration against his body as he lay flat. Slowly he sighted the disintegrator at the top of the level under which the man had crouched for cover, and waited for his next leap. Within him he felt only a bitter cold which matched the wind whipping above him.

Again the man moved—but he had crept to the side of the stairs before he leaped, and Rynason's shot bit into the stone beside him as he rolled to safety. Now only one level separated them.

Further down the stairs, Rynason saw the others moving up behind the smaller man. Still more were moving out from the other buildings and darting to the stairs. But he had no time to hold them back.

There was silence, except for the wind.

And the man leaped, firing once, twice. The second beam took Rynason in the left wrist and spun him off-balance for a moment. But he was already firing in return, rolling to one side. His third shot took the man's right shoulder off, and bit into his neck. The man staggered forward two steps, trying to raise his stunner again, but suddenly it clattered to the floor and he crumpled on top of it. A pool of blood spread around him.

Rynason moved back to the cover of the side wall, and watched for the other men. The first one had got too near; Rynason hadn't realized how easily they could approach in this near-darkness. He felt the numbness of the stunnerbeam spreading nearly to his shoulder; his left arm was useless. Cursing, he trained the disintegrator along the line of the steps and fired.

The disintegrator cut through the stone as though it were putty, for a range of twenty feet. Rynason played the beam back and forth along the steps, cutting them down to a smooth ramp which the attackers would have to climb before they could get to him.

One of them tried to leap the last few levels before Rynason could cut them, but he sliced the man in two through the chest. The separate parts of the man's body fell and rolled back to the untouched levels below. He had not had time to utter even a cry of pain.

For a time, now, there was complete silence in the wind. Rynason could see the inert legs of the last attacker projecting out over the edge of the third level down, and undoubtedly the others saw them too. They were hesitating now, unsure of themselves. Rynason stayed pressed to the stone floor, waiting. The wind whipped in a rising moan through the upper reaches of the building.

Another of the men slipped over the edge of the massive stairs, hugging the deeper darkness at the side of the stair-wall, and slowly inched his way up the newly-flattened ramp. Rynason watched him coldly, through a grey haze of fury which was yet tinged with despair. What use was all this, the killing, the blood and sweat and pain? It disgusted him—yet by its perverse senselessness it angered him too.

He cut a swathe through the crawling man, through head and neck and back. A gory shell-like hulk slid back to the foot of the ramp.

And abruptly the remaining men broke and ran. One of them rose and stumbled down the steep levels of the stairs, heedless of his exposure; with a shock, Rynason saw that it was Rene Malhomme. Another followed...and another. There were almost a dozen of them on the stairs; they all broke and ran. Rynason sent one beam after them, biting a depression into the rock wall beside them. Then they were gone.

Rynason moved back from the head of the stairs and leaned wearily against the stone. His left arm was beginning to tingle with returning circulation now; he rubbed it absently with his good hand and wondered if they would try the sheer walls on the other side of the Temple. He had scaled one of these ancient walls, but would they try it? Certainly they stood little chance coming up the stairs, unless they gathered for a concerted rush. And who would lead such a suicidal attack? These men were vicious, but they valued their lives too.

Yet he couldn't watch the black walls. Leaving the stairway unguarded would be the most dangerous course of all.

In a few minutes the hand-radio, forgotten on the stone floor behind him, flashed an intermittent light which caught his eye in the dusk. That would be Manning.

Rynason slid the radio over to the head of the stairs and switched on there, keeping an eye on the stairway.

"Lee, do you hear me?"

"I hear you." His voice was low and bitter.

"I'm coming in to talk. Hold your God damned fire."

"Why should I?" said Rynason,

"Because I'm bringing Mara with me. It's too bad you don't trust me, Lee, but if that's the way you want it I won't trust you either."

"That's a good idea," he said, and switched off.

Almost immediately he saw them come out from behind the cover of a fallen wall across the dusty street. Mara walked in front of Manning; her head was high, her face almost expressionless. The cold wind threw dust against their legs as they crossed the open space to the base of the steps.

Rynason stood motionless, watching them come up. Manning still had his two stunners, but they were in their holsters. He kept behind the girl all the way, pausing before pushing her up the open ramp at the top, then moving even more closely behind her. Rynason stood with the disintegrator hanging loosely in one hand at his side.

On the colonnade Manning gripped the girl by her undamaged arm. He nodded to one of the doorways into the temple, and Rynason preceded him inside.

As they entered Manning lit a handlight and set it on the floor. The room was thrown into stark relief, the shadows of the motionless aliens striking the walls and ceiling with an almost physical harshness. Manning paused a moment to look at the Hirlaji, and at the altar across the room.

"We can hear each other in here," he said at last.

"What do you want?" said Rynason. There was cool hatred in his voice, and the knife-scar on his forehead was a dark snake-line in the hard glare of the handlight.

Manning shrugged, a bit too quickly. He was nervous. "I want you out of here, Lee, and I'm not accepting any argument this time."

Rynason looked at Mara, standing helplessly in the older man's grip. He glanced down at the disintegrator in his hand.

Manning drew one of his stunners quickly, and trained it at Rynason's face. "I said no arguments. Put the weapon down, Lee."

Rynason couldn't risk a shot at the man, with Mara in front of him. He carefully laid the disintegrator on the floor.

"Slide it over here."

Rynason kicked it across the floor. Manning bent and picked it up, returned the stunner to its holster and held the disintegrator on him.

"That's better. Now we can avoid arguments—right, Lee? You've always like peaceful settlements, haven't you?"

Rynason glared at him, but didn't say anything. He walked slowly into the center of the room, among the Hirlaji. They paid no attention.

"Lee, he's going to kill them!" Mara burst out.

Rynason was standing now next to the interpreter. The handlight which Manning had set on the floor across the room was trained upwards, and the interpreter was still in the darkness. He lowered his head as if in thought and switched on the machine with his foot.

"Is that true, Manning? Are you going to kill them?" His voice was loud and it echoed from the walls.

"I can't trust them," Manning said, his voice automatically growing louder in response to Rynason's own. He stepped forward, pushing Mara in front of him. "They're not human, Lee—you keep forgetting that, for some reason. Think of it as clearing the area of hostile native animal life—that comes under the duties of a governor, now doesn't it?"

"And what about the men outside? Did you put it that way to them?"

"They do what I say!" Manning snapped. "They don't give a damn who they kill. There's going to be fighting here whether it's against the Hirlaji or between the townsmen. As governor, I'd rather they took it all out on the horses here. Domestic tranquillity, shall we say?" He was smiling now; he had everything in control.

"So that's your purpose?" Rynason said. There was anger in his voice, feigned or real—perhaps both. But his voice rose still higher. "Is butchery your only goal in life, Manning?"

Manning stepped toward him again, his eyes narrowing. "Butchery? It's better than no purpose at all, Lee! It'll get me off of these damned outworlds eventually, if I'm a good enough butcher. And I mean to be, Lee…I mean to be."

Rynason turned his back on the man in contempt, and walked past Horng to the base of the ancient altar. He looked up at the Eye of Kor, dim now when not in use. He turned.

"*Is* it better, Manning?" he shouted. "Does it give you a right to live, while you slaughter the Hirlaji?"

Manning cursed under his breath, and took a quick step toward Rynason; his hard, black shadow leaped up the wall.

"*Yes!* It gives me any right I can take!"

It happened quickly. Manning was now beside the massive figure of the alien, Horng; in his anger he had loosened his grip on Mara. He raised the disintegrator toward Rynason.

And Horng's huge fist smashed it from his hand.

Manning never knew what hit him. Before he had even realized that the disintegrator was gone Horng had him. One heavy hand circled his throat; the other gripped his shoulder. The alien lifted him viciously and broke him like a stick; Rynason could almost hear the man's neck break, so final was that twist of the alien's hands.

Horng lifted the lifeless body above his head and hurled it to the floor with such force that the man's head was stoved in and his body lay twisted and motionless where it fell.

Afterwards there was silence in the room, save for the distant sound of the wind against the building outside. Horng stood looking down at the broken body at his feet, his expression as unfathomable as it had ever been. Mara stared in shocked silence at the alien.

Rynason walked slowly to the mike lying beside the interpreter. He raised it.

"You can move quickly, old leather, when there's a reason for it," he said.

Horng turned his head to him and silently dipped it to one side.

Rynason lifted the broken form of Manning's body and carried it out to the top of the steps leading down from the temple. Mara went with him, carrying the handlight; it fell harshly on Manning's crushed features as Rynason waited atop the huge, steep stairway. The wind tore at his hair, whipping it wildly around his head…but Manning's head was caked with blood. In a moment, the men from the town came out from cover; they stood at the base of the steps, indecisive.

They too were waiting for something.

Rynason hefted the body up over one shoulder and drew a disintegrator with the hand he had freed. Slowly, then, he descended the steps.

When he had neared the bottom the circle of men fell back. They were uneasy and sullen…but they had seen the power of the disintegrator, and now they saw Manning's crushed body.

Rynason bent and dropped the body to the ground. He looked up coldly at the ring of faces and said, "One of the Hirlaji did that with his hands. That's all—just his hands."

For a moment everyone was still…and then one of the men broke from the crowd, snarling, with a heavy knife in his hand. He stopped just outside the white circle of the handlight, the knife extended before him. Rynason raised the disintegrator and trained it on him, his face frozen into a cold mask.

The man stood in indecision.

And from the crowd behind him another figure stepped forward. It was Malhomme, and his lips were drawn back in disgust. He struck with an open hand, the side of his palm catching the man's neck beneath his ear. The man fell sprawling to the ground, and lay still.

Malhomme looked at him for a moment, then he turned to the men behind him. "That's enough!" he shouted. "*Enough!*" Angrily, he looked down at the crumpled form of Manning's body. "Bury him!" he said.

There was still no movement from the men; Malhomme grabbed two of them roughly and shoved them out of the crowd. They hesitated, looking quickly from Malhomme to the disintegrator in Rynason's hand, then bent to pick up the body.

"It's a measure of man's eternal mercy," said Malhomme acidly, "that at least we bury each other." He stared at the men in the mob, and the fury in his eyes broke them at last. Muttering, shrugging, shaking their heads, they dispersed, going off in two and threes to take cover from the wind-driven sand.

Malhomme turned to Rynason and Mara, his face relaxing at last. The hard lines around his mouth softened into a rueful smile as he put his arm around Rynason's shoulder. "We can all take shelter in the buildings here for the night. You could use some rest, Lee Rynason—you look like hell. And maybe I can put a temporary splint on your arm, woman."

They found a nearby building where the roof had long ago fallen in, but the walls were still standing. While Malhomme ministered to Mara he did not stop talking for a moment; Rynason couldn't tell whether he was trying to keep the girl's mind off the pain or whether he was simply unwinding his emotions.

"You know, I've preached at these men for so many years I've got callouses in my throat. And one of these days maybe they will finally figure out what I'm talking about, so that I won't have to shout." He shrugged. "Well, it would be a dull world, where I didn't have a good excuse to shout. Sometimes you might ask your alien friends up there, Lee…what did they get out of choosing peace?"

"They didn't choose it," said Rynason.

Malhomme grimaced. "I wonder if anybody, anywhere, ever will. Maybe the Outsiders did, but they're not around to tell us about it. It's an intriguing question to think about, if you don't have anything to drink … what do you do, when there's nothing more to fight against, or even for?"

He straightened up; the splint on Mara's arm was set now. He settled her back in a drift of sand as comfortably as possible.

"I've got another question," Rynason said. "What were you doing among those men who came at me on the steps earlier?"

Malhomme's face broke into a wide grin. "That was a suicidal rush on you, Lee. A damned stupid tactic … a rush like that is only as strong as the weakest coward in it. All it takes is one man to break and run, and everybody else will run too. So it was easy for me to break it up."

Rynason couldn't help chuckling at that; and once he had started, the tension that had gripped him for the past several hours found release in a full, stomach-shaking laugh.

"Rene Malhomme," he gasped, "that's the kind of leadership this planet needs!"

Mara smiled up from where she lay. "You know," she said, "now that Manning is dead they'll have to find someone else to be governor…"

"Don't be ridiculous," said Malhomme.

THE END